A Harmony Falls Novel

Crashing the Congressman's Wedding

ELLEY ARDEN

author of *Save My Soul*

CRIMSON
ROMANCE
F+W Media, Inc.

This edition published by
Crimson Romance
an imprint of F+W Media, Inc.
10151 Carver Road, Suite 200
Blue Ash, Ohio 45242
www.crimsonromance.com

*To my brother who by example gave me enough
courage to step on stage. I cherish every hour we spent
at the piano, belting out show tunes.*

Acknowledgments

I am greatly influenced by music. The basic concept for this book came from a couple questions prompted by a popular song. My questions were, "What kind of woman stands up and stops a wedding, and what kind of groom runs off with the wedding crasher?" After much thought, my answer became *Crashing the Congressman's Wedding*.

The heroine and I share a profound respect for community theatre. The caliber of performances entertaining theatregoers in towns big and small throughout the United States simply dazzles. I urge you to support your local arts community. From performers to musicians to set designers and costumers, chances are there is immense and powerful talent wherever you live just waiting to hear your applause.

CHAPTER ONE

Alice shoved her feet into rhinestone-studded pumps, checked her teeth for smudges of red lipstick and dashed out the door onto the porch. She had exactly twenty minutes to get to church. Digging into her late mother's beaded clutch, Alice cursed her missing keys and walked as she rummaged, wishing a chat with the mail lady hadn't put her behind schedule.

Ruff. Mouse ran a zigzag pattern across the front yard, brushing filthy fur against her toile skirt.

"Stop it. You're dirty." Alice waved the dog away, but he brushed by again, causing her to stumble and step in a pile of …

"Crap!" She threw her handbag to the ground and stared at the clump of brown on the tip of her shoe. "Are you serious?" She tossed her head back and roared at the cloudless sky. "You've got to be kidding me."

Stomping her way back to the porch, she kicked off the shoe and scraped the toe in the too-tall grass. Dog doo smashed between the rhinestones. Alice growled, dropped the shoe to the ground and limped into the house, heading straight for her only other pair of remotely matching heels…character shoes. Wearing beige stage shoes wasn't the fashion statement she hoped to be making today, but she didn't have a choice. She was already late, and the only place to buy shoes in Harmony Falls was the thrift store, which was closed for the congressman's wedding.

These were the moments when Alice missed her mother most. She kissed fingertips and pressed them to Mama's face, smiling at Alice from behind dusty glass. "Tough day, Mama. Wish you were here."

With a frown, Alice hastily fastened the shoes, leaving too much slack. At least the whole day hadn't been a bust. Shirley had delivered mail early on account of the wedding, and in her hand was a letter from the Arts Foundation. Alice's application was a finalist, which put her one step closer to opening an honest-to-God theatre in Harmony Falls. No more *The Sound of Music* in the park pavilion. No more *Peter Pan* in the church social hall. No more Poor Little Alice Cramer, the girl with impossible dreams.

She sighed and then smiled, determined not to let the bad parts of the day drown out the good.

Ten minutes remained, and Alice still had no idea where to find her keys. For all she knew, Mouse stole them again so he could chew on her lucky rabbit's foot. When she rolled her eyes, she noticed her brother's keys hanging on the hook by the door where he'd left them when he rode off with a group of deadbeat friends. Her nose crinkled. Charlie's car smelled like cigarettes and was littered with trash, but it would get her to the church faster than walking.

Snagging the metal off the hook, Alice tiptoed through the grass (careful not to step in anything questionable) and scooped her purse from the front yard before plopping into the driver's seat of Charlie's car.

"Ouch!" She dug a hand underneath yards of scratchy skirt and pulled out a tiara. The glistening crown was pretty. A bit odd, too. And it definitely wasn't hers. She tossed the headpiece into the backseat and shook her head. How Charlie managed to get any woman into this car willingly was beyond Alice. She kicked aside empty paper cups, shut the ashtray, rolled down the windows and pressed pedal to the floor all the way to church.

Making it with a few minutes to spare, Alice paused at the back of the sanctuary, smiling down the lily-lined aisle at the smoking hot man standing before the altar. His tuxedo was tailored, his shoulders were back and his hair was impeccably groomed. He'd worn the same lift to his blond bangs since high school. Back then, the fashionable hair blended with city-bought clothes to make him look even more privileged than he was. Now, almost fifteen years and two professional titles later, the flip of his bangs made her smile, because she recognized it for what it was—who he was—a predictable, responsible, creature of habit.

Alice sighed, smoothed a hand over the snug bodice of her dress and tried to remember a time when she didn't love Justin Mitchell.

He saw her then, and she dug deep into her theatrical bag of tricks to smile with a sincerity that would charm sight-challenged ladies in a theatre's back row. He bought it, smiled back, and Alice imagined the fine lines crinkling around his green eyes. The breath she tried to take stuck in her too-small throat, and she remembered she needed to walk, needed to move, needed to take her place. This wasn't the time for longing or regrets. This was a wedding.

The man she loved was getting married.

But he wasn't marrying her.

Alice released the misery with a shake of her head and then scanned the noisy crowd for friendly faces. Ken and Carole Flemming sat three pews from the altar, three pews too close to the fire, with an empty space between them where Kory should be. Today of all days, Alice missed her best friend, but resident doctors didn't get time off for non-family weddings—even if those weddings featured small-town royalty.

Sucking a mouthful of air, Alice took a step down the aisle. Although she preferred Mrs. Flemming's quiet smile to the rambunctious fawning of just about everyone else in town, for once in her life the attention that went along with a walk down the center aisle wasn't appealing. Alice chose relative anonymity in the back of the church instead.

She slid into the pew and studied the groomsmen, imagining her brother in the mix. Aside from Will and Mark Mitchell, Charlie knew Justin longest; he deserved to be up there, too. She closed her eyes and pictured Charlie cleaned up, with his bow tie tilted and his boutonniere hanging off his lapel. But when she opened her eyes, he wasn't there. Congressman Mitchell couldn't take the risk. Bonds of childhood friendship were no match for the potential embarrassment of having a drunk at the front of the church.

Alice's stomach clenched as she wondered if Charlie was sober today—wherever he was. If not, she prayed he stayed safe and out of too much trouble. She'd been praying for that a lot lately. And she'd keeping praying and hoping it wasn't too late, that Charlie wouldn't end up like their father.

The thoughts tugged acid into Alice's throat, and she held a hand to her mouth. Dropping her shoulders on a heavy exhale, her head followed. Too much emotion for one day. A loose piece of silver thread hung from the bottom of her skirt, and she felt tears that had nothing to do with the thread.

If it weren't for the false eyelashes and extra coats of mascara, she'd have allowed herself a good cry. Justin was getting married, and although she knew this day would come, the finality hit hard.

She sniffed, dabbed beneath her eyes with her knuckles and lifted her head, smile firmly in place. The church teemed with people who had every reason to celebrate. Congressman Justin Mitchell, chief financial officer of Mitchell Company, Inc., was making good on his late father's promise to bring life to this dying town. His congressional term set the stage for tax breaks and corporate-friendly zoning, and his arranged marriage would align the two most powerful families in the state. It didn't hurt that as a wedding present, the bride's uncle promised his new plastics plant to Harmony Falls.

So Alice loved Justin. Big deal. Who was she to stand in the way of progress?

Maisy Carmicheal twisted in her pew. "You look lovely, dear." She smiled at Alice and adjusted her cotton candy pillbox hat. For a beautician, the woman wouldn't know style if it stole her ugly hat and slapped her upside the head. "Wait until you see the bride. Perfection. My best updo ever."

"I'm sure." Alice held her eyes firmly in place despite the urge to let them roll down the aisle. Of course Morgan Parrish was perfect. Her father was the mayor. His power and money made certain she was skinny, educated, and flawless—everything Alice wasn't.

More tears burned the backs of Alice's eyes, but before a drop could fall, a flash of red passed on the Alice's left. Josie Parrish stopped beside Maisy's pew. "The combs aren't holding," she hissed. "Help me, Maisy. This is a disaster. I can't believe she lost that tiara. I told her that bachelorette party was a foolish idea."

Tiara? Hmmm. Alice watched the bride's mother grab Maisy around the wrist and pull her out of the sanctuary. *A tiara.* Like the one Alice sat on in the front seat of Charlie's car? *No.* Alice couldn't imagine Morgan ever stooping low enough to accept a ride from the likes of Charlie. And why would Charlie have been anywhere near Morgan's bachelorette party?

Alice shook her head. The tiara in Charlie's car couldn't be the same tiara Morgan was missing. Besides, after all the years of friendship, Charlie would never hurt Justin.

But a drunk Charlie did things a sober Charlie would never do.

Alice winced. Absolutely not. She refused to believe it. This was just an uncanny coincidence. And yet…how many tiaras were floating around Harmony Falls?

She looked at Justin. He held his hands waist high and alternated squeezing palms, first the right on top and then the left. From the back of the church, she couldn't see him clearly, but she bet he was chewing his bottom lip. He always chewed when he was worried. She couldn't shake the feeling that maybe he had something to chew about.

A few minutes later, Maisy returned to her pew. "Just a little hair snafu, but I worked my magic. The bride is officially breathtaking," she said, gloating loudly enough for several rows to hear.

Alice fidgeted, trying to push thoughts of missing tiaras out of her head. She scratched at her tight bodice, picking at a hard piece of plastic that ran up her side and dug into her right breast. When she did, her elbow bumped the man sitting next to her.

"You look pretty, Alice." The Mitchell's ancient gardener smiled and tipped his hat. "Just like Marilyn Monroe."

"That's sweet, Tubby. Thank you." Never mind that the dress was about as comfortable as a potato sack. She didn't remember it being so itchy when she wore it last year in *Hello, Dolly*. Then again, with no operating budget for her twice-a-year productions, the dress hadn't been dry-cleaned since.

Alice sighed again. Maybe borrowing a dress from the costume closet wasn't the best idea, but her alternatives weren't any better. Wear a frock from the thrift store or drop a bundle on a trip to the city and a dress she'd never wear again. In all honesty, this was hardly the occasion to splurge. She'd have worn black if she thought she could've gotten away with it.

Tubby started humming show tunes under his mint-scented breath, and Alice wondered if he recognized the dress. She slipped down in the pew, wishing she could hold her head up high, wanting just once to attend a Mitchell affair without sitting in the back with the outcasts. But Johnny Cramer made sure his daughter knew her place. Even though he died years before Mama, his words rang clear: "When they look at us, all they see is trash, baby. The sooner you realize it, the better off you'll be."

Yeah? Well, Alice realized it—and she was tired of waiting for the better-off part. All she needed was the grant money, and she'd have a real brick and mortar theatre. She'd know her place then, and everyone else would know her place, too.

Alice Catherine Cramer belonged in the spotlight, not in the audience. She deserved applause, not pity. And with that little pep talk, she smiled, fidgeted again and pressed her back to the uncomfortable pew.

A crinkled hand landed on her leg. "Maybe I'm the only one who thinks it, but that boy's making a mistake." Tubby shook his head. "A man should be happy on his wedding day, and he's not happy."

Alice blinked. Her mouth fell open, and she almost agreed, but before the words tumbled out, trumpets blasted through the church, and Molly Lunsford, cousin of the bride, tossed a handful of rose petals over the white runner near Alice's pew. She looked like a cherub with ringlet curls. The crowd oohed and aahed, and the child bowed. After another handful of petals hit the ground, the little girl sprinted down the aisle toward her papa, where he scooped her into his arms and planted a kiss to her cheek.

Sweet. Alice stole a glance at Justin. Despite the precious child and chuckles from the pews, he was somber, and his misery made her heart hurt. Before she could dwell too much on Justin's lack of happiness, creampuff bridesmaids strolled past, each one stuffier and stiffer than the next. Alice didn't know most of them. They were outsiders, Morgan's friends from a fancy law school in Connecticut, with poufy hair, chandelier earrings and bright pink lips. They looked like the cast of *Willy Wonka* threw up all over the stage.

And then Morgan appeared. The only thing missing was the choir of angels. She was five foot ten with hair of spun silk and a designer dress flown in from France. Whatever the Parrish family had paid for all those layers of lace, they paid too much, Alice thought, smoothing her hand-me-down dress over clenched thighs. She imagined all the overpriced clothes Morgan would buy with the Mitchell family money. What a waste.

The Justin Alice knew wasn't like that. He spent his money, drove new cars, and owned nice homes, but he gave a lot of his money away, and he looked best in blue jeans and a faded Penn State hat with the brim brushing his neck. Morgan wanted to change him, starting with the push to move to D.C. and the "for sale" sign in Justin's front yard. If the banshee got her way, Justin would turn into suit-and-tie-wearing Congressman Mitchell full-time and leave Harmony Falls for good.

As much as the thought depressed Alice, his complete transformation was for the best. When Plain Old Justin was around, Alice couldn't breathe. The lines blurred. He didn't seem so off limits wearing faded jeans and a crooked smile, and she didn't feel so unworthy. In those moments, dreams of being together spilled into her days, and she wasted time walking around a fool in unrequited love.

Thankfully, it'd been a long time since Alice had been stuck in the "I love Justin" rut. She was happy with the direction her life was headed. After today, she hoped the rut would be permanently patched. A girl could dream, couldn't she? Yes, she could. Even if those dreams weren't likely to come true.

A trumpet blast startled Alice as Morgan floated down the aisle with her nose in the air. Alice refused to fawn over a bratty bride, so she focused on the groom instead. His face lengthened and two shadows slashed his cheeks. There wasn't an ounce of joy in the man.

Smile, Justin. Although it would hurt Alice more to see him smile, even the smallest sign of happiness would set her free with the knowledge that at least one of them was getting what they wanted. The idea that he harbored second thoughts pushed her to the edge of the pew.

Smile, Justin. She willed her thoughts over the terrible trumpeting.

But Justin wilted further. There was no shine, no sparkle, no… tiara.

Alice gasped. What if the tiara in Charlie's car was Morgan's? What if they…? She slapped a hand over her mouth. Charlie had been known to romance anything with the right parts, and Morgan's parts were in demand. If Charlie had been drunk, it was possible he made a move.

Oh, God. Alice bit the inside of her cheek. She'd been called a drama queen more times than she could count. Was she being overly dramatic now?

While the Parrish side of the wedding party beamed, the Mitchell side paled. Even Mark, the youngest and goofiest brother, looked worried. And why shouldn't he be? Everything was wrong. This wasn't a wedding march, this was a funeral dirge. The black cloud that appeared over Harmony Falls the day Justin's daddy died had grown into a full-blown storm with Justin directly in its path. And he didn't deserve to be. He was a good man who spent his days helping everybody else. Now it was time for somebody to help him.

The honorable thought carried Alice to her feet. She gulped a few mouthfuls of air, trying to gain courage. "Stop." The shaky command travelled a few pews.

Half the church looked at Alice instead of the bride.

"Can I talk to Justin?" Alice spoke louder this time, pushing out of the pew and into the aisle. "It'll only take a minute. I promise."

Alice hadn't heard so many gasps since she fell off the pavilion stage into the shrubs during opening night of *A Chorus Line*. But she kept her eyes on a gaping Justin, and blocked out the rest.

"Daddy, she's ruining my wedding."

Mayor Parrish stepped in front of his whining daughter and cut off Alice's view of the groom.

Alice stopped cold, watching the mayor move closer. "Justin, I..."

A couple hands wrapped around her upper arms, and Alice felt tugged from behind. "Let's go, little lady. No time for drama. This here ain't a thee-a-ter."

Alice didn't know whose hands were dragging her from the church. Frankly, she didn't care. Her character shoes caught on the runner as Mayor Parrish turned to console his daughter, and that was when Alice saw Justin, his mouth still hanging open.

"She's missing her tiara." Alice looked away from Justin and over the gaping crowd. "Charlie has it." Her voice cracked.

"Get out," Morgan screeched.

The next thing Alice knew, heavy doors shut in her face and Gilbert Hoover plopped her on a cement step. "Go home, little lady. Fix yourself some tea. It'll be all right. You'll see."

What did Gilbert know about all right? He pumped gas for a living. He lived in a doublewide. The pancake breakfast was his idea of gourmet "eats." This town was mad, and she was neck-deep in their insanity. Well, no more. It might be honorable to help a man who was making a terrible mistake, but from now on, Alice Cramer was only helping herself.

Justin could marry the banshee. Alice was going home. She lifted her skirt and stomped barefoot down the church steps.

"Where're your shoes?" Gilbert called.

It seemed her dignity wasn't the only thing Alice left lying in the aisle.

• • •

Justin stared at his beet-red bride-to-be as she cowered in her father's arms. Strands of inky silk slid from her hair combs and stuck to her wet cheeks. "What's going on?"

She burrowed deeper into her father's chest. "Alice is crazy."

Maybe. Charlie's little sister had done a lot of crazy things in her life, but standing up in church without good reason seemed extreme, even for a Cramer.

Between Morgan's sniffles, Justin could've heard a boutonniere pin drop in the stricken church. He glanced at his mother, sitting stoically in the front pew. No doubt she figured he had a plan to get the situation under control. But for the first time since his father died, leaving the job of diplomacy to him, Justin was at a loss for words.

He should probably start with an apology to his mother and permit her the *'I-told-you-so.'* She'd warned him time and time again about the damage Charlie could do to his reputation. He glanced at Morgan, picturing her missing tiara sitting atop her head. Apparently she didn't get the same lecture.

Sickness swirled in Justin's stomach, and a flash interrupted his speculative trance. The bright light drew his attention down the aisle to a large man with an even larger camera taking photos of the twirling flower girl. At least someone was having fun. But as soon as the sarcastic thought faded, another more ominous thought formed. That man, that camera, could ruin Justin by capturing an unsavory, unscripted moment and putting it on display.

Justin's chest clenched. He had a choice to make. He could either go through with what he once thought of as a politically advantageous wedding solely to save face and as a result, risk life with a duplicitous woman, or he could step back, take a breather and make certain he was doing the right thing by marrying a woman he didn't trust and didn't love simply to follow through on his father's promise.

With an inhale and an exhale, Justin raised his hands. "I need a minute."

"Don't you dare walk out on me," Morgan threatened through clenched teeth.

He hadn't thought about walking out until she suggested it, and now that she had, he wanted to. Walking wouldn't solve the big problem, but if he walked, nobody would see him blow. And for the first time in years, he heard the ticking of a time bomb with each beat of his heart.

Months' worth of frustration trapped between his cummerbund and bowtie. He'd allowed himself to be a pawn in a game his father started years ago. There were no more clandestine whiskey and cigar meetings between Marvin Mitchell and Robert Parrish, but their plans for power remained. If their dreams for political dominance had died along with Justin's father, Justin wouldn't be standing here today. But he was standing here, a willing accomplice, because as Marvin's oldest son, it was his duty to follow through with his father's best-laid plans, plans which included a Congressional seat and a loveless marriage.

Crazy? Maybe. But his father said powerful families arranged marriages all the time. They were business transactions of mutual benefit. In this case, Justin would get a beautiful, poised, politically-appropriate wife, who happened to come with a dowry of several hundred million dollars in the shape of an international plastics plant, and Morgan would get a wealthy husband with power, influence and title. Everybody won, unless, of course, you counted love, which Justin didn't. Love didn't win elections. Love didn't balance the measly budgets of rural Pennsylvania towns. Love was one of the few luxuries powerful people couldn't afford.

Or so he'd been told over and over again by the most unlikely source, his bride-to-be. He'd been focused and methodical about marrying Morgan for the power and stability her family could offer this town, and yet he stood here, shaken by the unknown. Was it possible Morgan had risked his reputation and all they planned to accomplish together by carrying on with Charlie?

When Justin looked at Morgan, she looked away.

On the first wave of impulse Justin had permitted in years, he threw up his hands. "I apologize, but this isn't going to happen today."

"I'll kill her," Morgan roared. So much for poise under pressure.

Any other time, Justin would've placated her for the sake of keeping appearances, but now he simply wanted to get away. He walked up the aisle with gasps and gossip to his back. He could only imagine his mother's fear and confusion. It was almost enough to turn him around. Almost.

"When I get my hands on that little…" Morgan's threats against Alice faded and somewhere in the distance a door slammed.

Justin didn't stop to see what happened. At the moment, he was too numb to care. His mind warned that this could be political suicide, but he needed the truth. Once he knew what Alice knew, he could form a plan.

He reached down to scoop up the pair of shoes that littered the aisle. Alice Cramer had given him grief since the day they first met. She had better have a damn good explanation now.

CHAPTER TWO

Justin sat in his parked car in the Cramer's driveway, lifting his bowtie like a noose and scratching the back of his neck. He'd get his answers, warn Alice to watch her back around the Parrishes, and then he was out of here, out of town, somewhere quiet where he could think.

Road tripping in a tuxedo wasn't his idea of comfort, but he wouldn't waste time stopping by his house, risking a run-in with Morgan and her parents. Absolutely not. He had nothing to say to them, which meant just enough time for one stop before he hit the highway and headed for his intended honeymoon destination, seven days at his condo on Carolina Beach. If the squeezing muscles in his shoulders and neck were any indication, he was more desperate for the getaway now than he had been the day he planned the trip.

Justin bounced his forehead off the steering wheel and sighed. For somebody who spent his adult life trying to do right, he sure ended up with a lot gone wrong. Some paragon of community service he turned out to be.

Shelving the self-pity, he pushed out of the car and set off in search of answers. His heavy feet trudged over the uncut lawn and to the front porch where Mouse met him with a whine. The mutt wiped a lip-load of slobber across Justin's tuxedo pants. "Hey, boy. It's been awhile. How you been?" Justin rubbed the dog behind the ears.

Mouse pressed his wet nose to Justin's jacket pocket and snorted.

"Those aren't for you. Just some fancy mints."

The dog yapped a blast of rancid air at Justin's face. "On second thought…" He reached into his pocket, pulled out the wedding favor and ripped open the netting. "Sit."

Mouse whined again, but he sat long enough for Justin to drop three mints between two rows of yellow teeth.

"Good, boy." Justin patted the dog's head before he reached for the screen door handle.

When Mouse lifted the torn edge of the screen with his nose and dashed inside, Justin paused. Twenty years ago, he would have followed, but tonight he should knock.

After the third knock and no answer, he pushed inside. "Alice?"

The dog replied with a deep snort of Justin's jacket pocket. "No more, boy. They're all gone."

He stepped around the dog, walked between two discolored couches and ducked beneath an archway into the empty kitchen. The same bowl of fruit he'd been robbing apples from for decades perched on the mint green counter top. There were no apples now, not since Mrs. Cramer passed away. Now the bowl was filled with snack bags of Doritos. He shook his head and smiled.

"Alice, we need to talk."

There was the possibility she didn't go home after the drama at the church, but the door was open and the lights were on. He only hoped the Parrishes didn't somehow get here first.

Leaving the kitchen, Justin stepped down a long hallway lined with outdated family photos, and passed Charlie's old room. A few more steps and he stuck his head around a peeling doorjamb. He noted the same pink shag carpet, the same floral wallpaper, the same canopy bed. Only the bed looked much smaller with her grown-up body sprawled atop the ruffled comforter.

"Alice?" He walked to her, tucked a yellow curl behind her ear and smoothed a hand over her bare back.

She sniffed, rolled over and a bottle of whiskey fell to the floor. Eye makeup smeared across her cheek. "You got married."

"And you got drunk." He hoisted an arm around her waist and pulled her to his side. "Sit up. We need to talk."

"I'm not drunk. I'm…you got married. Charlie. The banshee. Tiara." Her voice trailed off.

Mouse howled in the other room, and all but Justin's churning gut froze. The sense of doom told him it was only a matter of time before Morgan and her parents came looking for Alice. And in Alice's current state, the confrontation wouldn't be pretty. Justin wished he didn't care. Alice assumed the consequences by standing up in church. He didn't want to defend her. He wanted answers.

Mouse barked again, the sound fading into the distance as the dog no doubt bolted across the lawn after whatever—or whoever—raised the alarm. A blast of acid burned Justin's throat, and he let Alice fall out of his arms on to the bed. He shouldn't have come. If the Parrishes blocked him in the driveway, he'd be trapped in the eye of the storm. With all this adrenaline coursing through his veins, Justin couldn't guarantee his usual poise.

The screen door rattled.

Justin looked to the rectangular window, hugging the low ceiling. He wondered if he was strong enough to hoist himself up and out before someone came in.

"Charlie has a tiara," Alice slurred, struggling to sit. She reached out, steadying herself by smashing Justin's cheeks between her palms.

The screen door banged again.

Maybe it was Charlie…Justin didn't want to face the man who slept with his fiancée any more than he wanted to face Morgan and her parents, but Charlie would have answers, too.

"Did you hear me?" Alice spoke clearer and louder now, blowing puffs of whiskey across Justin's face.

"Shh." He pressed a finger to her lips, straining to hear movement in the other room.

A rattle. A rustle. Two quick sniffs. Mouse exploded from the hall and leaped onto the bed.

A sickening heat crawled over Justin's face as he struggled for a normal breath. This damn dog would be the death of him.

Alice rested her weight against the pooch, while the dog's enthusiastic tail pummeled Justin's side. His unsteady breathing mixed with the thumps of the tail and the whimpers from Alice, but otherwise, no ominous sounds drifted in from the hall.

Justin tried again, shoving an arm behind Alice's back, pulling her to sit. "We need to talk."

"Talk." She swayed, and then she sighed. "No, sing." She must've downed the bottle in three gulps to be this drunk this fast.

She clutched the lapel of his tuxedo and belted out a sloppy tune about the sun. Justin sorely doubted the optimistic lyrics.

Growling in frustration, he stood. He wasn't going to get a damn thing out of her but more aggravation for him. How long would it take her to sober up?

Justin paced the shag carpeting, breathing deeply, trying to calm his nerves. He had options. He could leave and find Charlie, get the answers there. But where to look for Charlie and whether or not he was any more sober than his sister made it an unappealing option.

Justin yanked on his bowtie. He could go home, lock his doors, shut off his phones and brood until he felt calm enough to face the situation head on. But talking to Morgan and trusting whatever she'd say wasn't appealing, either. And God knew he didn't want to face his family so soon after leaving them to clean up his mess at the church. He winced. All along he'd wanted a plastics plant, not a wife. Now he was about to end up with neither.

Mouse yelped and, hurdling Alice's lifeless body, raced by Justin and into the hall. Any progress Justin made at slowing his heart rate flew out of the room with the dog. Every muscle in his body contracted, pumped full of adrenaline. Fight or flight. Justin took a step toward the door. When Alice moaned, he glanced back. She knew something, something that would help him understand what happened in the church and what should happen now.

Mouse reappeared, tail wagging, snorts of playfulness rustling Justin's pants. The jumpy dog was going to give Justin a heart attack before he got a coherent word out of Alice.

With all his muscles cocked and loaded, it was only a matter of time before Justin strode across the room and scooped her into his arms. "Come on, Alice. We need to talk." Mouse barked again. Justin couldn't concentrate in this constant state of fear. "But not here."

"Why?" she whimpered.

"People are coming."

"What people?"

"Angry people. Come on. I need you to walk." He helped her to her feet.

"Why are people angry?" She fell to the floor in a boneless heap, Mouse yipping beside her.

Another adrenaline surge and Justin took control, lifting her into his arms where she snuggled her face to his neck. He squeezed his shoulder to his ear to stop the tingles.

"You got married." She sniffed.

"No…I didn't." His strong strides down the hallway made him too winded to say more.

She squirmed until he had no choice by to drop her on her feet in the living room. "What did you say?" She grabbed fistfuls of tuxedo to keep her balance.

Justin looked over her head, out the screen door and into the front yard. His car idled in the driveway. If they could make it there before anyone else showed up, he could drive in relative peace, giving Alice plenty of time to sober up and provide answers.

"We'll talk in the car." He grabbed her hand and pulled her to the porch.

"Where are we going?"

"I don't know." But he couldn't stay here with all this rush and worry in his head, and she shouldn't stay here, not in her condition, not when she couldn't defend herself should irate Parrishes arrive to exact revenge.

Mouse yelped and nipped at Justin's pocket.

"He's hungry." Alice dropped to her knees, resting her weight around the dog's neck.

Justin slammed his hands through his hair and stared into the graying sky. "Charlie can feed him."

"Charlie's gone."

The pooch ran toward the porch, and Alice gave chase, tumbling to the lawn. Justin flashed his eyes between the ragged pair. "Where's his food, Alice?"

She giggled in the grass as the dog raced by. "At the store."

"What do you mean at the store? Don't you have any here?"

"Nope." Her lips sputtered on the "p" sound.

Justin growled as more adrenaline juiced his veins. Forget it. Here he was standing in the Cramer's front yard, the ringmaster to Alice's circus, when what he needed to be doing was getting the hell away.

Thunder rolled. Justin glanced at the darkening sky and shook his head. It figured. When it rained, it freaking poured. He looked at Alice. Her head had fallen to the side. Her eyes were closed. Her chest rose and fell rhythmically. No matter how much and how fast he wanted to get away, he couldn't leave her passed out on the lawn in the middle of a thunderstorm.

He stepped toward her as the first drop fell and lightning lit the sky. No wonder the dog was so spooked. Justin dragged the drunken drama queen into his arms, and another drop fell. Then another. With a long exhale and a burn in his thighs, he hoisted her off the grass. By the time he took his first step, the sky unleashed.

Son of a bitch. Justin breathed through gritted teeth as rain pelted his face. When lightning flashed again, he flinched and adjusted her in his burning arms. Only after he deposited her onto the passenger seat and closed the door did he see the dripping dog at his side.

Mouse's tail wagged despite the miserable weather.

"Go inside, boy," Justin yelled above the pounding rain. He pointed to the house for emphasis, but the dog only circled him as he crossed in front of the car, heading for the driver's seat. Another lightning flash, and the dog yelped.

"Fine. Fine!" Justin hollered, opening the back door for the mutt. He regretted the slipshod decision the minute he caught sight of wet paws and overgrown claws on flawless leather. But what else could he do? It was too late to change course now.

By the light of another crackling bolt, Justin pulled onto the country road. Water dropped off the ends of his hair and slipped down the sides of his nose while his heart hammered in his chest. If that weren't enough misery to handle, his throat clenched at the stench of wet dog while his hands strangled the wheel. *Holy hell.* What had he done?

Alice snored beside him. Her head pressed against the passenger side window, and her feet disappeared beneath her dress. He'd planned to drive around until she sobered up, but at this rate, she'd sleep for hours.

He glanced at the gas gauge. *Hours.* The tank would be empty by then. *Hours.* He groaned. He didn't have hours to waste. He should've formulated a plan by now, figured out a way to neutralize what happened at the church, finagled a way to get the plastics plant without compromising his principles by taking a cheating woman for his wife.

Maybe he'd drive until the rain stopped and then dump Alice and the dog back home whether he had answers to his questions or not. But first, he needed gas.

Five miles down the lonely country road, he slowed at a stoplight and glanced at the gas station. Between the windshield wipers' frantic swipes and the splatters of relentless rain on the windshield, Justin saw the Parrish Lexus parked alongside Pump Six. He locked his jaw, tightened his hands around the wheel and blew through the light, heading out of town.

With the gas gauge needle buried in red, Justin finally stopped for gas two towns over. While Alice slept, he bought Mouse some beef jerky and an air freshener for his car, and then he sat as the car idled, staring at droplets on the windshield. He was screwed. Morgan would never admit to cheating on him, so no matter what Alice knew, it was a Cramer's word against a Parrish's word, and that wasn't even a contest where public opinion was concerned. Morgan had never made a misstep—at least not one that she'd ever been caught in. Alice and Charlie? The list of missteps was too long to count.

Justin dropped his head to the headrest and closed his eyes. When Mouse stuffed his head into the center console and nudged Justin's hand, Justin patted the dog's damp fur. "Now what, buddy?"

The dog didn't answer. Of course the dog didn't answer. Justin opened his eyes and scowled at the sunroof. The fact that he was disappointed that the dog didn't answer only highlighted his dysfunctional state of mind. And through it all, Alice slept, like nothing remotely unnerving had happened. A red mark peeked out from beneath her cheek where her face met the door. The strange tilt of her neck made him wince. She was going to wake up hung over and hurting.

Justin shrugged out of his tuxedo jacket, balled up the still-damp cloth and, reaching past the dog, shoved the jacket beneath

Alice's head. She whimpered, and a strand of hair curled into her mouth. He leaned closer to tug the curl from her lips. His heart throbbed in his throat. Even with four vents blasting cold air in his direction, he was on fire. It'd been a long, strange day, and he had no idea how to make it right.

Justin resettled into his seat and gripped the wheel. He dreaded going home without a plan of attack, but he couldn't drive around aimlessly. With a sigh of defeat, he guided the car from the parking lot to the road where he caught sight of a reflection in his headlights. A road sign. Interstate 79. That's where he wanted to be. Headed to Carolina. Nobody would find him there.

His body reacted to thought as though a decision had been made, and his foot tramped the gas pedal. As the car rocketed up the highway ramp, Justin knew he was crazy. Dragging Alice Cramer and her mangy mutt to Carolina was the ultimate proof. When he blew by the next exit without turning around, he feared the lunacy was permanent.

Through it all, he kept breathing, kept driving, hoping the monotonous journey would calm his heart and the quiet would inspire his mind. With any luck, the panic was temporary and he'd have a grip on his emotions and a solid plan by morning.

He hoped so.

When Alice woke up sober and saw what he had done, there'd be hell to pay.

• • •

Alice opened her eyes, and she could've sworn she saw a big old sign that read "Welcome to Carolina Beach." With her eyes closed again, she lamented the funniness of dreams, sometimes so vivid they seemed real. Smells and all.

Beef jerky. Yum. She hadn't had a stick in years, not since her daddy died.

She rolled to her side, and pain shot through her shoulder. *Ouch!* She tried to sit, but something tightened against her chest. The struggle caused her head to spin and her belly to lurch.

"Hey, sleeping beauty."

That voice. She pried her dehydrated eyes open as her head whirled and her stomach churned.

"We'll be there in ten minutes or so."

Justin. Alice groaned. "Where…what…why?" The words acted like an elixir, causing memories to flash. The church. The tearful walk home. The "tea."

"Oh, no." Alice cringed.

"Oh, yes." Justin reached over their heads and opened the sunroof.

Humid August air stole a bit of the staleness from the vehicle, but not enough to help Alice feel better. She grabbed the opened bottle of cola from the center console and finished it off without asking permission. As the carbonation fizzed in her throat, the fog in her head dissolved. "You didn't get married?"

"Nope."

"Because I stood up?"

Justin dragged a loud breath into his open mouth and then pushed an exhale through loose lips. "What do you know about the tiara?"

"Not much. I sat on one in Charlie's car. It was so odd, and then you looked so sad. I…" Alice watched his knuckles whiten as he death-gripped the wheel. Another wave of nausea surged into her throat. She pressed a fist to her lips. "Oh, God, Justin. I'm so sorry. What if I'm wrong? What if it's not hers? Or what if it is, but there's a perfectly rational explanation for it being there? I didn't think things through, and I…oh, God." The tears felt good. Maybe they released some of the alcohol.

Justin drew another labored breath and shook his head. "I looked at her, really looked at her, and she couldn't look back.

The longer I looked at her, the angrier I got, because if there was a rational explanation, she would've given it to me at the church. Something didn't add up."

Reality trickled into Alice's sleepy brain. He wasn't married. She watched early morning sunlight dance across his face. He was here. With her. In…Carolina Beach? "Where are we going?"

"On my honeymoon."

Alice suddenly preferred the blackened state of drunkenness over her current reality.

He laughed, but the skin around his eyes didn't crinkle and his lips didn't hitch. And then he started to chew. He stared out the windshield, shaking his head and gripping the wheel like he was afraid to lose control.

"Why am I here?"

He bristled at her question, and she was no longer certain she wanted to know. But it was too late. Leaning an elbow on the window ledge and scraping a palm across his lips, Justin released a low growl. "I figured you had answers. But then you were too drunk to talk and I sort of…" His shoulders drooped. "I couldn't leave you like that."

There was more to the story. Alice could tell by the way he chewed his lip.

"You couldn't leave me drunk in my own bed?"

He scowled. "Morgan threatened you."

"She wasn't serious."

"You don't know that." But he didn't look particularly concerned. He'd stopped chewing and stared out the windshield, looking more tired than worried.

Still…"Do you think she was serious?"

He took longer to answer than she hoped. "Probably not, but her father can make your life miserable by interfering with the theatre opening. Maybe with you out of town for a couple days, they'll have time to cool off where you're concerned."

Fat chance. If the Parrishes blamed her for the botched wedding, running off with Justin wasn't going to help. Then again, she hadn't "run off" willingly.

"You're kidnapping me."

He shook his head. "I'm rescuing you from a bad situation."

Alice balked. Of course he was. Always the hero, even if rationalizing his heroics meant twisting the truth. "Whatever helps you sleep." She shook her head and stared out the passenger window. "What about Parrish Plastics?" Which was supposed to be his most heroic accomplishment to date.

"That's a bit complicated now. But don't worry. I have a plan."

He always did.

"When I get to the beach, I'm going to call Harold Parrish, and we're going to discuss the plant like the educated businessmen we are. He can't build anywhere else on U.S. soil for less, thanks to me and my work in Congress. He's a smart man. He wants a successful corporation more than he wants a married niece." She looked in time to see him punctuate the words with a crisp nod. Alice couldn't help but think he looked like he was trying to convince himself. "Harmony Falls will come out of this unscathed. I truly believe that."

Who was he kidding? He was speeding down the highway with a Cramer in his car. "What about your precious reputation? Will that come out unscathed, too?"

He winced. "People break off engagements every day. I have to believe it's better to call it off now than to be married to her amidst rumors of her infidelity. How capable would I look if my wife was running around on me? Who would support me or my projects then?"

Alice closed her eyes and leaned against the cool window. She was exhausted from more than the liquor and unsatisfying night's sleep. Justin exhausted her. All this talk about reputation and image and his ability to emotionally disconnect from the most brutal experiences in the name of his "projects" annoyed her.

"What about my project?" she whispered without opening her eyes. Two weeks ago she'd asked Justin to talk to people on the grant committee on her behalf. She was so damn close. Before this. She had a sickening hunch things were different now.

"Alice, after what happened in that church, if I stick up for you or the theatre…"—he glanced at her, wrinkling the muscles of his face—"…people will talk."

She narrowed her eyes. "People are already talking. They've always talked. They always will. Whatever." She waved a hand. "I don't care what anyone says. I wasn't the one who cheated, and I didn't ask to be here." She glared at him. "But since you care, don't worry about helping me. I can fight for my theatre without you."

Congressman Mitchell's heroics were better saved for people who needed to be rescued. Alice Cramer rescued herself years ago, and she wasn't about to step back into old habits, old habits that led her to feel ashamed.

She twisted until her upper body stretched between the seats, her hand groping the backseat and floor while Mouse dove around her sweeping arm. "Where's my purse? I'll rent a car and drive myself home. Then you can ride your white horse back into town without so much as a speck of dirt on your face, and you can walk down the aisle like nothing *compromising* ever happened. Tell everyone Alice Cramer is crazy. The tiara was a joke. Tell them…" Her hand met nothing but empty space.

"Where's my purse?" Alice spoke slowly, sitting rigid, glaring at him.

"I only grabbed you and the dog."

"Crap." She slumped against the leather and huffed some more. "I want to go home. I want a do-over. I want to close my eyes, wake up and realize this is all a bad dream."

It sucked to be the kind of girl who never got what she wanted.

CHAPTER THREE

Bringing Alice Cramer on what was supposed to be his honeymoon wasn't just a bad dream, it was a cold, harsh nightmare turned reality. And now Justin was going to have to deal with the repercussions.

He parked his car in a spot marked with the number fifteen and let his eyes linger on the mirrored high-rise. "It's oceanfront." The fact gave him immense pleasure when he'd purchased the condo as an escape from the pressures at home and work. Now, it didn't produce a twinge of satisfaction.

"Good for you." She wasn't happy.

He couldn't blame her. This wasn't exactly his best plan. Hell, this wasn't planned. This was what he got for letting impulse lead the way. He gave her a sideways glance again and bit down extra hard on the inside of his bottom lip. If only he'd thought this through…Looking at her now, the danger was clear. Despite her ugly mood, she was beautiful, so beautiful he had to look away.

All those years, Justin had kept his distance for one reason. Alice Cramer wasn't the right kind of woman. Untamed starlit curls drew a man into her spotlight, and the ensuing chaos of her family life threatened to bring the man down. A Mitchell couldn't take that risk. And yet, here he was…with the vanilla scent of her perfume stealing every last bit of fresh air from his car.

He threw open the door and took a deep breath. "I'll grab the suitcases. You head into the lobby. Hopefully we won't be seen." He didn't expect to be recognized hundreds of miles from home, but he'd taken enough chances already.

As he rummaged in the trunk, Alice wandered away from the car. When he flung the last bag over his shoulder, he saw her disappear around the corner of the building—in the opposite direction of the double doors.

What now? Why couldn't she be simple, easy, uncomplicated? Why the drama all the time?

"Hey," he called after her, glancing back at the dog staring at him from the back seat.

With a huff, Justin dumped the bags in the trunk and restarted the car to give the dog some cool air. Then he set out to see what sort of trouble Alice was getting into.

He found her neck deep in the ocean.

Alice jumped a wave, and Justin was assaulted by a flash of creamy skin and black lace. She was swimming in her underwear. Catching sight of a pile of clothes out of water's reach, Justin shook his head. Apparently, she had ditched her dress. Why was he not surprised?

"What are you doing?" he called above the surf.

She flashed him a smile he hadn't seen in years. "I've never been to the ocean."

His untucked shirttails whipped in the wind, and with the strength of his hands he fought the chaos. "I guess that explains it."

She stayed smiling, considering him with the same hypnotic eyes he knew as a child. Back then, he wondered what she saw when she looked at him. Now, he was afraid to know the answer.

"I'm going to get the bags and the dog out of the car, and then I'll bring you a towel. Be careful. No further. You hear? In fact, stay closer to the beach. The undertow is strong, and I'd like to avoid another rescue."

A few steps up the beach and her wail hit his back. "I don't need to be rescued."

But she did. Somebody had to keep her from making rash decisions, like stopping weddings and swimming in the ocean half-dressed. He slowed his pace and closed his eyes. That someone couldn't—shouldn't—be him. On an inhale, he opened his eyes and returned to the surf. "Fine. No more rescues."

"Good, because I'm not a baby. I can take care of myself. Stop telling me what to do. Stop treating me like you're my father or my brother. You're not. You're just a guy. I'm just a girl. And you make life too complicated." She raised her arms to her side and fell backwards into the sea.

Justin's heartbeat quickened as he searched the choppy water, waiting for her to surface. Her father died an alcoholic and her brother looked destined to follow. Not being lumped in their category was a good thing, but where did that leave him?

Relief flooded him when her head broke the surface. She pushed soggy curls from her face, and raising her arms over head, spun until a wave knocked her off her feet. She was definitely not a baby. But if he was just a guy and she was just a girl, then bringing her with him was an even bigger risk. He had obligations, expectations and an image to uphold. In trying to avoid a scene at the church, he'd put himself in one hell of a compromising situation.

The cell phone resting in his pants pocket vibrated like it had so many times on the drive down. He watched Alice play in the waves as he listened to messages. Two calls related to the agricultural committee he served on. One call came from an aide, congratulating Justin on his marriage. One was from an arts council member, returning his call about Alice's application. There was one message from his brother, Will, one from his brother, Mark, two from Morgan, and only four from his mother.

Justin felt a growing guilt over not being man enough to spare them all this pain by calling off the charade months ago. He'd come close on a couple occasions, but Morgan caught on and appealed to his sense of obligation. A responsible man didn't propose and then renege. He worked on the relationship. A responsible man didn't walk away from the opportunity to bring hundreds of jobs to a town in desperate need. He made choices and stood by them. He honored his father's memory.

Standing in the sand, eyes glued to Alice, Justin's guilt multiplied. He wasn't a responsible man. He embarrassed his family, and he jeopardized the plastics plant. And now he stood on a beach in North Carolina watching a beautiful woman—who wasn't his new wife—frolic in the sea.

The bottom corner of his BlackBerry dug into his palm, numbing the skin and sending a shot of pain up his arm. He didn't loosen his grip. His fingers wrapped tighter around the black box, and he wondered how much pressure it would take to crush it. How long would it take for the world to stop turning without access to him? It was a melodramatic question. Surely he wasn't as important to everyone's success and survival as he'd allowed himself to believe. But something inside of him withered at the thought of testing the theory.

Alice floated on her back, further out to sea, and all Justin could imagine was the scandal that would result from her drowning on his watch.

"You're asking for trouble, Alice," he yelled. "Come closer to the beach."

She flipped into an upright position and glared at him. "*You're* asking for trouble if you keep telling me what to do."

He didn't want any trouble. His intentions were good. Keep Alice from being dragged to sea. Get Alice out of Harmony Falls so she could sober up, he could get answers and tempers could cool. Marry Morgan and complete his father's lifelong mission of bringing industry back to town. But would Harold Parrish care about intentions? Would he go through with his promise to build the plastics plant even though Justin backed out of marrying Morgan?

"Seriously, Justin. What are you doing? Go get the dog before it gets too hot…or I'll do it myself." She started to rise from the water, dripping wet. The stringy straps of her black panties rode low on her hips.

Justin groaned. "I'm going. I'm going." He took a few steps back. "Get back in the water."

She stopped knee-deep in the surf. "So now you want me to get swept away. You don't make any sense." Throwing her hands over her head, she turned and dove beneath a wave.

Alice was right. He didn't make sense—nothing made sense. His life was supposed to be straight and narrow. By winning back the congressional seat his father's death left empty, Justin was able to effect change where it mattered most, implementing steep tax cuts and generous incentives to corporations who set up in rural Pennsylvania. The congressional service was supposed to be temporary, but Justin surpassed everyone's expectations, and newer, loftier plans formed. The presidency? He laughed the first time Robert Parrish suggested such a thing. But these things took on a mind of their own.

Maybe Justin needed this break from the constant pressure and planning. Maybe the stress of the wedding and the wheeling and dealing at work had finally taken its toll. He was a young guy, but even young guys suffered high cholesterol and heart attacks. While his latest physical showed a healthy body, his mind went unchecked. Had the constant pressure caused this fissure in his normally practical thinking? If so, then a few days away from it all should smooth the crack.

Unfortunately, this wasn't a vacation. The circumstances were far from ideal. If he stayed beyond the few hours of sleep he needed to drive home to Harmony Falls, he'd have to face his age-old feelings for Alice, while he worried about what awaited them back home. Where was the peace in that?

Sun scalded his face as though he were in the universe's hot seat, but the blue sky kissing the horizon beckoned as pelicans floated above the crystal water on a steady stream of warm, salty air. Carolina Beach was a dream location—sun, sand, and solitude—the perfect place to clear his head and plot a plan that would allow him to face the mess back home, a mess that was messy enough already without including Alice.

She floated on her back, drenched in sunshine. Her eyes were closed. Her arms barely moved. Despite their sticky situation, she looked carefree. Justin craved that freedom, a freedom he would've had if his father lived longer and Justin could've grown at his own pace, made his own mistakes out of the public eye. There'd have been no overwhelming expectations and no one to answer to but himself. But that wasn't his reality.

"Are you going? Go! Feed him, too. He'll eat anything humanly edible."

She'd been awake for only a few hours in the last fourteen and already he had a headache. If he wanted any semblance of peace, he was going to have to rein her in. "So I can't tell you what to do, but you can tell me what to do?"

"Because you dragged me here. It's only fair."

"Like hell it is, Alice. You played a part in this, too."

She righted, tilted her head and wrinkled her nose. "A minor part. You're the star, buddy."

He shoved his hands in his pockets and looked beyond her to the water's edge. So much for reining. On a sigh, he conceded. "Do we have to bicker like this?"

"Under the circumstances, yes. This whole thing sucks, and I don't see how either one of us can say 'screw it' just to enjoy a couple days in the sun."

Nah. Justin had never said "screw it" to anything. "Screw it" was irresponsible. His face contorted under the weight of his thoughts.

"Plain Old Justin would've said 'screw it'."

"Who?"

"The man you used to be before…" She jumped a wave. "Never mind. Just go."

The man he used to be? Had the last few years of obligation and ambition split him in two? He glanced at the dusty tips of his patent leather loafers sinking in the sand, and flinched when his palm itched to brush them clean. So what if they had? Polish and rhetoric were required traits for a politician. Plain Old Justin remained. He just stayed out of Congressman Mitchell's way.

And damn if that didn't bother him as he carted the luggage up to the condo, fed Mouse a bowl of canned chicken, and debated his next move. Congressman Mitchell wanted to haul his biggest liability off the beach and out of eyesight, but Plain Old Justin pushed in another direction. He was at the beach. He'd been driving all night. A quick swim would wash away some of the sleep that hounded him and might even prove to Alice that he hadn't changed enough to deserve her disdain. Maybe then she'd calm down and stop yapping long enough for him to form an executable plan.

Moving swiftly, before the nagging voice in the back of his brain wrestled control, Justin tugged on trunks and led Mouse back to the beach, finding Alice where he'd left her, bobbing on the waves. He relaxed a tiny bit as the sun soothed his frazzled nerves. It was time to look on the bright side. At least he wasn't married. Sure, walking away from Morgan was a potential disaster now, but had he married her and endured years of treacherous behavior, there was no telling what sort of nightmare he'd be living.

Far enough up the beach to afford a little admiration, Justin didn't divert his eyes when Alice jumped a wave. If he was closer, admiring Alice would be problematic. Standing next to her he would see the water droplets sliding down the curve of her throat, diving into the valley between her breasts, and he might feel compelled to lift the bra strap that slipped down her soft shoulder and…A twinge tugged at the skin below his waist. He released a growly breath and adjusted his trunks. Maybe he wasn't far enough away after all.

She saw him then, jumped another wave and smiled. Her breasts bounced with the rest of her body, and he stared too long into the sun, sort of wishing it would blind him. He hung his head and let his shoulders sag. Once again, he felt the weight of the precarious position he'd put himself in. It had always been a precarious position where Alice was concerned.

She was fifteen the first time he told himself it was wrong to look. Back then, he was twenty-one, and a young man leering over the overdeveloped curves of a young teen amounted to perversion in most opinions. Her brazen attempts to attract his attention made matters worse. He looked once or twice—more like whenever he thought he could get away with it. But when he hit the campaign trail, ambition put an end to the unseemly temptation. No matter how beautiful she was, she was still a Cramer. Looking at Alice, seeing too much, feeling too much, and imagining more were luxuries an upstanding politician couldn't afford.

But Plain Old Justin had leeway.

Justin looked at Alice again and told himself the lacy undergarments were no different than a bikini. She was covered—barely—and he had to get a grip.

It'd be so much easier to do if she had something decent to wear.

Forcing himself to stare at her until the warning bells in his head quieted, Justin splashed through the surf and stood waist-deep at her side. "We need to get you some appropriate clothes."

Her narrowed eyes stuck to his chest. "When you say that, I hear your mother's voice in my head. *Appropriate*." She squinted up at him and wagged her head in a humorless mock. "The heroic, do-gooder thing is old. You're nothing but an uptight prude. There's no difference between this and a bathing suit."

Alice stepped back and drove a stiff arm into the water, splashing him in the face.

"Stop it." Justin swiped at the barrage of droplets, stinging his eyes.

She did it again.

"I said, 'stop'." He clenched his teeth together and felt the muscles in his neck contract.

She did it again.

He didn't recall directing his body to act, but it did, diving into the waves and winding his arms around her waist. He dragged her under, water searing through his nose and burning his throat before he raised them above the water as quickly as he'd pulled them under. They surfaced with her back pressed against his belly and her arms pinned to her side. He squeezed her there, feeling her chest rising and falling as he struggled for his own breaths.

"Let go!" She pushed her head against his breastbone and kicked her legs out, forcing them deeper.

Justin tried to gain leverage with his feet and fired the muscles in his thighs with her bottom pressed against them. But when the sand slipped, so did he.

Alice got away before the water drew him under. A cold current blasted him without her body as a shield. When he surfaced, she was several feet away in waist-deep water, shaking her head in his direction. "Have you lost your mind?"

He dragged a painful breath through his mouth and into his lungs, holding it there, hoping rationality would seep in. "You splashed me first."

She dragged her palms from her forehead over her hair to the back of her neck, stretching her breasts toward him. "That wasn't very congressman-like."

When she said *congressman*, she tightened her voice until the tone was condescension personified. He couldn't help but chuckle.

Dragging his gaze from her breasts, Justin gulped more air. "My apologies. I'm not sure how I'm supposed to act, considering our colorful history and the fact that…" *I left one woman at the altar and am leering at another.*

"I knew it!" She drove a hand into the water again, this time splashing away from him. "I knew this would get weird. You'd bring up stupid things I said and did when I was younger. Well you know what? You don't need to worry about a replay of our *colorful* history. Not only am I mad at you for making matters worse by bringing me here, I stopped liking you years ago. There's not much to like these days."

The sun beat against his cheek, leaving a burn on his skin like he'd been slapped. "Is that so?"

"Yep. You've changed."

"Here we go again." He rolled his eyes. "Of course I've changed. So have you. Everybody changes."

"Yeah, but you changed into an entirely different person, Congressman Mitchell."

There went the condescension again. And there went her arms, crossing her chest, forcing mounds of flesh higher.

He was surrounded by water, but his mouth had never been so dry. He tried to focus on her words instead of her lingerie-clad body. "I take it you don't like my title."

"I don't care what you call yourself. You could call yourself Emperor. It's how you act that matters. If you call yourself Emperor but act like Plain Old Justin, then that's cool—weird, but cool. Same with Congressman."

She tossed her head around the title with enough attitude to freeze the Atlantic. He wished the water would freeze; specifically, freeze him from the waist down.

"Let me get this straight. You have a thing for Plain Old Justin, but not Congressman Mitchell?" Against his better judgment, he trudged toward her.

She backed up. "I don't have a thing for any part of you." She flinched, and he didn't think it had anything to do with her squinting into the sun.

"You're supposed to be a good actress, Alice."

"And you're supposed to be a married man."

That hit below the belt, accomplishing exactly what he hoped the cold water would do. He needed the reminder, because while he wanted peace and time to think, he didn't want enough distance that he forgot who he was and the mess he'd come from.

Maybe it was the sun. Maybe he swallowed too much salt water. Alice waded out of the ocean where a beach towel defused some of the heat her body threw his way, giving him time to breathe deep and stop whatever was left of the stirring below his waist. He waded out of the water too, keeping himself busy, picking up the discarded dress, throwing the extra towel around his neck and whistling for Mouse.

Alice walked ahead, her bottom swaying against the towel. It was a side of her he knew well. She'd been turning her back on him for a long time, turning her back as he turned her away.

"Who knows you're here, and do they know I'm with you?" The towel slipped off her shoulder, carrying a bra strap with it. She had her hands shoved underneath her armpits, forcing the flesh of her chest to bulge.

Justin drew a shaky breath through his lips and redirected his gaze to the dog racing ahead of them. "Will knows I'm here, but he'll keep quiet. He said no one's seen you since the church. I told him you were probably with Kory."

Alice gasped. "You lied? *You* lied. I thought you were like George Washington. Huh. You're just like all the other politicians, aren't you?" She shook her head. "And now you're dragging me into something else I don't want to be a part of. I guess I have to call Kory and make her an accessory to this crime, too."

He wished Alice would quit reminding him of her discontent. He got it. She was ticked. She didn't like him—at least she didn't like Congressman Mitchell—and she didn't want to be here with him. But they didn't have a choice. Even if he was rested enough to jump in the car and drive home, without a solid plan, he'd be doomed.

"I don't want to bring Kory into this anymore than you do, but what's the alternative? I need a couple days, Alice, and then I'll have a plan in place." He ignored the pinch of doubt squeezing his brain. "There's no phone in the condo, so use my cell to call her while I shower."

She seemed to consider his words, watching her feet shuffle through the sand. And then she looked at him with one side of her mouth curved in a way he hadn't seen in years. She used to preface every wayward hijinks with a half-smile that warned of her mischievous intent. She'd been a study in mood swings all her life. Apparently that part of Alice Cramer hadn't changed.

"A long time ago, I would've snuck into that shower with you." She sighed and gave her head an admonishing shake. "It's a good thing I don't like you anymore."

With that, she took off running ahead of him, her feet kicking up sand, the towel slipping below the band of her black bra.

Damn it if he didn't wish he could turn back time.

CHAPTER FOUR

Kory, with her warped sense of humor, loved the idea of Alice shacking up with the good congressman while the town reeled from his no-go wedding. Obviously Kory didn't understand the seriousness of the situation, but Alice did. One look at her sopping wet reflection in the mirrored closet doors, and she saw the gravity written all over her face. She was going to rot in hell for standing up in that church. And hell was spelled H-A-R-M-O-N-Y-F-A-L-L-S.

Three short knocks on the door rattled Alice's already shaky nerves.

"I'll be right there," she called, clutching Justin's cell phone to her chest as she turned to scan the room for the suitcase he mentioned. A couple pieces of shiny black luggage rested on the tiled floor beside the bed.

That was not her luggage.

Alice tossed the phone to the mattress and hoisted the largest suitcase onto the bed, somehow managing not to drop her bath towel. With a zip and a lift, she opened the bag and stared at its perfectly pressed contents.

These were not her clothes.

Three more knocks punctuated the pounding of her heart. "Alice, the clothes…"

"Go away, Justin."

She pulled a pair of jeans from the suitcase. They were the longest, narrowest pair of jeans she'd ever seen.

He knocked again. "I didn't pack for you. This wasn't planned. Remember?"

How could she forget? He planned to honeymoon in North Carolina with his appropriate, politically approved wife. These conservative pieces of overpriced clothing were no doubt the banshee's. And now, they were Alice's torment. She bent forward and sniffed the air rising from the suitcase. The spicy scent burned the lining of her nose and tossed her stomach. Not only did the clothing look like Morgan, it smelled like Morgan. How was Alice supposed to get past the stench? How was she supposed to resurface in town dressed in Morgan's things? It wouldn't work.

Dropping the bath towel, Alice struggled to pull on her still-damp underpants and bra. As she did, she studied her shape in the full-length mirror. Tubby said she looked like Marilyn Monroe. Blonde hair. Big boobs. Huge hips. She could see the resemblance. Too bad the modern world didn't appreciate women with curves. She looked back at the jeans stretched on the bed. Long. Straight. Narrow. Everything she wasn't. Why bother?

Alice glanced around the room again, her tired eyes settling on the fluffy white comforter folded over at the top to reveal pinstriped sheets. The plump bedding called to her with the promise of sound sleep and a false escape from this horrible situation. She almost gave in. But slipping into Justin's guest bed dressed in nothing but her bra and panties seemed seedy. Even so, her skin pimpled, aching for the brush of cotton.

He knocked again, scattering her goose bumps. "Please, go away, Justin."

"I need my phone."

She grimaced, knowing she couldn't stay sealed in this room. Sooner or later she was going to have to let him in. "Just a sec."

Ripping a white blouse from the suitcase, Alice huffed and puffed as she struggled with tiny buttons, finally shoving her arms through the sleeves. The fabric stretched across her belly. Tight, but the first three buttons fastened. And if it weren't for her breasts, the next three buttons would've fastened, too. Instead, she looked like the star of a pornographic office parody with breasts spilling like water balloons from the open collar of a conservative shirt and black lace panties covering her bottom half. All she needed were the wire rims and a pencil to chew.

God, how she wished she were rehearsing for a silly play instead of starring in her own psychological thriller. She pictured herself on stage instead of stuck in Carolina. She ached for her theatre, the protection from her past, the promise of her future, the sense of wonderment in the chilly, dusty, dimly lit air. But with sunshine blasting her face from the open blinds, it was useless to pretend she was anywhere but here…with him. She growled and swiped at her image in the mirror, not hard enough to hurt herself, but hard enough to rattle the sliding door.

"Are you okay?"

She wasn't surprised at his concern. Justin probably thought she needed to be rescued again. He was forever the hero, swooping in to guide the lesser man—or woman. It wouldn't be half as annoying if he hadn't already rescued her so many times before… her eighteenth birthday when one kiss to her cheek convinced her to go back to school and earn her GED. She hated that memory, hated how hopeful that kiss made her feel. False hope. He was good for that. Like the hope he gave her when he said he'd "pull some strings" to help with the theatre grant. Look what had become of that. Nothing.

Swiping at her tears, Alice snatched the cell phone off the bed. She wasn't going to mope. She didn't need to be rescued. Besides, there was no rescuing her from her current humiliation. As if the day could get any worse, now she had to tell the man of her dreams that she was too damn fat to fit into his fiancée's clothes.

With a breath through her open mouth and her gaze locked on the popcorn ceiling, Alice cracked the door and shoved the cell phone toward him. "The clothes aren't going to work."

"Are you sure?" His fingertips tickled her skin as he retrieved the phone.

Alice growled. "I'm sure."

"Did you try everything?"

"I don't have to."

"Yes, you do. You don't have another option unless you want to wear your dress."

If she thought the dress she wore to the wedding was itchy before, she could only image climbing into it now, after wind on the beach had doused it with sand.

"Seriously, if the pants are a little long, roll them up," he continued. "No big deal."

She yanked open the door, giving him a first-rate look at the ill-fitting blouse. "What do you think the odds are that something's going to fit better than this?" She waved a limp-wristed hand down the side of her body.

Justin blushed. He rolled his eyes to the ceiling and then turned and walked away. "Do what you want, Alice. You always do."

Not true. Otherwise she'd be running across the room, launching herself onto his back so she could strangle him. Being here, this close to him, was killing her.

She slammed the door, putting a barrier between them, and determined not to leave the room until he was ready to leave the beach, and then she would…Alice glanced out the glass sliding doors to the balcony where her party dress flung over the railing, ruffling in the breeze. She would have to wear the dress home—scratching from sand, smelling like fish, looking in no way, shape, or form like she'd spent the weekend in Chicago with her best friend. But who would care? Alice Cramer was always doing crazy things.

Her stomach flipped as she dropped to the bed. Who was she kidding? She would care. Years spent in a family whose name was the punch line to town jokes made a girl more than a little neurotic about her actions. That's why she could kick herself for standing up in that stupid church.

She opened her mouth to guzzle enough air to calm her panic. What was done was done. Now she had to figure a way out of this mess.

Alice glared at the suitcase of doom. What were the chances something in there would fit? Slim. Slimmer than the banshee. But Alice gave it another try. She hated the idea of Morgan laughing at her expense.

After too many pressed white blouses to count, Alice found a stretchy tank dress at the bottom of the suitcase. The item no doubt hung on regal Morgan Parrish, but on busty Alice Cramer, the dress looked like a second skin. Alice winced, rolled her shoulders back and sucked in her stomach like Coke through a straw. It didn't help. She exhaled and stuck her tongue out at her reflection. Screw it. She was covered. This dress would get her out of this room, out of this condo and one step closer to home.

Grabbing a scarf from the ransacked pile of clothes, Alice tied the colorful fabric around her waist to hide the little pouch that lived below her belly button. She blew air through her lips to loosen the worried lines on her face and pulled her wet hair into a nub at the base of her neck. A couple uncooperative curls dangled at her temples. Good enough. After all, Justin wasn't someone she wanted to impress.

A strange flutter tripped along her esophagus and trapped inside her throat. She ignored it, reaching for the knob. Her hand shook, which was harder to ignore. The tremor made her think twice about facing the man in the other room. He stirred things in her she would rather not feel, causing anger to become her protective shield. Anger wasn't good for her current outlook on life. She had pledged to be optimistic as a rule for the sake of her theatre. That's where she needed to keep her focus. That's where she needed to be. If she stayed in this room, she couldn't go home.

With chin lifted and shoulders back, Alice opened the door. "I'm ready."

Justin leaned against the kitchen counter in khaki shorts and a linen shirt unbuttoned below the dip in his throat. One look at him and she salivated. Her fingernails dug into the wooden door as she struggled to keep from slamming it shut again. Damn him for looking like the man she loved, kind, decent, uncomplicated and tempting as hell. Damn her for refusing to let go of the stupid fairytale. Her muscles flexed, readying retreat.

"I forgot to give you these." He walked toward her, lifting a hand from behind his back, dangling her character shoes from his fingertips. "I tripped over them on my way out of church."

He stopped a foot away, splashing her with a crisp clean scent that was decidedly Justin. She held her breath and looked to the shoes, noticing his wrist. A thick cord of muscle travelled up his tan arm until it merged with his bicep. Mercifully, that muscle, a muscle she'd felt harden beneath her hand a time or two, remained covered by his sleeve.

She jumped her gaze to the gentle swell of his chest, closed her eyes for a moment, breathed—just a bit—and reached for the shoes. "Aren't you a regular Prince Charming?" She resisted the urge to ask him if he came to see if the proverbial shoe fit. They both knew it wouldn't.

As he transferred the shoes to her hands, he stepped closer, fanning his fresh scent over her face. She gulped and fought the impulse to step closer still, where she could bury her head in his neck and breathe him in until he'd become so much a part of her they couldn't go their separate ways. Stupid thought. Thoughts like that got her into trouble years ago. She wasn't looking for trouble now.

With a roll of her shoulders and a tip of her chin, she looked at him, catching him raking his eyes over her body turned breakfast sausage in Morgan's tight dress. She fidgeted under the weight of his stare. "Don't look at me like that."

"I'm…sorry. We need to get you something decent to wear."

Decent. She had news for Congressman Mitchell. It didn't matter what she was wearing, she'd never be decent enough for him. And that made her flinch. She glared at the ground, kicked a foot behind her and shoved a heel in place. "You poor baby. It must be agony to see me in Morgan's clothes after she wore them so…*decently.*" Alice stumbled over the extra saliva in her mouth.

After kicking the other foot behind her to slap on the other shoe, she marched back to the mirror for one last look—needing a minute to shake off her shame.

But Justin followed. "All I meant was…"

"I'm fat." She wrinkled her nose at the reflection in the mirror.

"You're not fat."

"Okay, then you're blind." The dress was a size four. Alice wore a ten on a very good day. She wanted to kick him and then punch him until he hurt as much as she did. Being dragged off in the middle of the night was bad enough, waking up guarded and embarrassed was even worse, and now she had to endure contemplation and criticism until he came up with a suitable plan to salvage his precious reputation which was marred by their unseemly association. God, what a freaking mouthful! Alice dry heaved.

She stormed past him, but not before he snaked an arm around her waist. At the jolt of intimate contact, she froze, back to his belly, his hot breath ruffling the hair on her head. His arm slashed a line of heat below her breasts, leaving her thighs to quake.

"You make me so angry," he whispered, never loosening his grip.

"Ditto." It was lame, but when talking about what feelings they brought out in one another, anger was the only safe one on the list, especially when he was touching her like this.

His hand shifted, smoothing over her stomach. Her vision blurred. Impulse picked at her skin, urging her to rub against him, reach back and graze a palm up his leg. But she couldn't move with his fingertips burning a trail along the thin elastic of her underpants.

"I think you're beautiful." His mouth was inches from her ear.

She crumbled, tilting her head so his breath could warm her neck and sprinkle tiny thrills throughout her body. Maybe he was lying, but to what gain? She didn't know. All she knew was it was pathetic to pine for an unattainable man like this. But knowing didn't make it any easier to stop.

He turned her to face him. With his eyes closed, he dropped his chin to his chest on a labored exhale. It was weird. Creepy almost. Like he wasn't fully in control of what he was saying or doing. Even that couldn't keep her body from tingling and priming for any number of outlandish things. His kiss. His caress. His body entangled with hers.

At some point, while she watched the struggle play out on his wrinkled face, her brain wrestled control from her body. In an instant, her every muscle tensed, fighting the tide, reminding her that the tide wasn't good. It smacked of long-ago desperation, false hope, and this time Alice refused to play the fool.

When Mouse whined and scratched the front door, she recognized an escape. "He has to pee."

Before Justin uttered a word, she left the room and grabbed the dog. She was determined to erase the memory of the last five minutes and undo the damage Justin had done to her resolve.

"Okay," he called after her.

But it wasn't okay. None of it was okay. Standing up at his wedding had been her biggest mistake. Bringing her on his honeymoon had been his. And now he'd gone and trumped both those mistakes by touching her and confessing something he should've taken to his grave.

I think you're beautiful. She shook away his words, unwilling to risk her heart again. And he shouldn't be risking anything on her. Not that he would, or even could. He might think she was beautiful, but no amount of beauty could trump her last name. Cramers and Mitchells were different people, going different places.

Alice would have no trouble remembering that if they weren't currently stuck in the same place.

• • •

Justin didn't follow Alice when she disappeared with the dog. He wanted space—needed space—because the longer he was with her, the more irrational he became.

She talked down about herself. So what? Big deal? What woman didn't want to change something about her body? If he had a penny for every time Morgan droned on about her flawed manicure or shiny T-zone, he could buy Parrish Plastics out from underneath Harold and guarantee the damn thing stayed in Harmony Falls forever. But something about the way Alice attacked herself didn't allow Justin to stay quiet.

And not staying quiet was a big mistake.

He'd opened a mess of emotions. He was sure of it. Otherwise, she wouldn't have run out.

So he waited for her return, sliding open the screen door and dragging a patio chair to the edge of the balcony with every intention of forming a solid plan to get them out of this hellish situation sooner rather than later. Instead, with his feet kicked onto the railing and his legs crossing his ankles, he fell in and out of restless sleep to the rhythm of the waves. One minute he dripped a cold sweat, dreaming about lifting Morgan's bridal veil, and the next minute he breathed heavy, dreaming about Alice, touching her, kissing her, listening to her whisper his name.

He needed to get a grip.

Standing, Justin stretched and made his way back into the condo, resettling on the sofa, out of the hallucination-inducing heat, where hopefully he could sleep without further rude awakenings, and wake up clear-headed.

Before long, he heard Alice's voice again …

"Justin?" She was standing above him. Sunlight split the pine boughs behind her and circled her head like a halo. Charlie lurked in the distance, cleaning the fish they caught earlier.

Justin smiled at her, eager to hear what she wanted, willing to give her anything before Charlie dragged him off to Sullivan's bonfire.

She adjusted her polka-dotted bikini top, giving him a show, dipping her finger in the edge and pulling the triangle low enough to show the contrast between her fresh tan line and a patch of milky skin.

He was getting hard.

"Justin? Open up."

Hey, that was his line.

"Are you hungry?"

Like hell he was. Reaching up for her, he wrapped a hand around her wrist, and when he tugged, she screamed.

Justin lifted his head…off the back of the sofa and saw Alice—clad in Morgan's awful dress—sprawled across his lap. No bikini. No creek bed. No pine trees overhead. He was in his condo living room with her belly resting on his thighs, her head twisting over her shoulder and her baby blues darkening with accusation.

She jumped up, straightened her dress and dropped a phonebook in his lap. "Jerk. I thought we might want to order pizza. You're such a…"

"I was sleeping, Alice. You don't wake a person out of a sound sleep to ask if they want pizza. I haven't slept in twenty-four hours."

"Yeah, well I haven't eaten in…a long time, and you have the money."

Roughing his hands over his face, he growled into his palms and forced air like steam out his nostrils. "We're leaving at sunrise."

"Fine." She thrust a hip, and her fist landed on her side.

"Good." He stood, towering over her.

"Exactly."

Justin pushed past her to the peninsula of granite breaking the kitchen and living area in two.

"Wait. Why? Did you come up with a plan, or did you get bad news? Is everything okay? Is my theatre okay? Did you hear something about the grant? Are you…"

"Alice, stop talking. Just stop. I don't have a plan. Yet. I'll figure it out on the drive home. What waits back there can't possibly be as bad as what's going on here." He pulled two twenties from his wallet and tossed them on the counter. "Order your freaking pizza. I'm going to bed."

She whizzed by him, blocking his way into the bedroom. "I don't know the address here."

He turned, snagged the builder's magnet off the fridge and threw it on the counter by the money. "There."

"There? That's all you have to say?" Her voice rose with each word. "Explain yourself."

"What are you talking about? I'm tired. Move." He grabbed her upper arms and started to lift.

She squirmed. "Put me down."

"Gladly." He deposited her to the side and stormed into his room.

Only she followed him.

"How are we going to do this? We need a plan. I don't have anything to wear. We can't just waltz back into town *together*. We should stagger our returns. How can we stagger our returns?"

That was when he noticed her hair, which had been pulled back in a knot at her neck, was now as wild and crazy as her sleep-deprived mood. No blown-dry loops of sunshine grazing her chin, instead kinky, frizzy springs poked out in all directions. And her nose was red, but not red like the lipstick her lips were missing. Her mouth formed a pale, hard line across her face, and her eyes jumped out at him. They were bold, blue and full of fury.

"Alice, go to sleep. We'll talk about this later. The exhaustion is getting to you."

She lunged, driving both fists into his breastbone, forcing him to trip on his own feet. He reached one hand behind him to shield the hard corner of the bedside table and the other hand to her waist to soften her fall should they both crash.

And they did. On the bed. With Alice on top.

She rolled off of him immediately, but she didn't jump off the bed like he expected. She also didn't hit him with her left hand, which rested inches from his right hip.

Justin was afraid to move, afraid to say a word, afraid to breathe should it pull her out of whatever peaceful trance she'd landed in. But after several seconds of eerie silence, curiosity won. Maybe she'd fallen asleep.

Turning his head, he watched her watch the ceiling fan rotate and wondered if this crazed state of sleep and food deprivation would give way to some sort of weird spiritual enlightenment.

"I hate you," she whispered.

So much for that theory.

• • •

Alice watched the fan blades whirl and wished she could close her eyes and make the man beside her go away. He was ruining everything. Years of building a wall strong enough to support her fragile indifference of him and strong enough to imprison her true feelings for him were wasted after five seconds by his side.

"I'm sorry you feel that way."

She told herself not to look at him, that he didn't deserve her attention, but something in his voice was so unlike the proud and sure voice of Congressman Mitchell. She had to see.

When she turned her head, he was looking at her, and if she didn't know any better she'd think regret was written all over his face. Regret about what, she didn't know. There was too much.

She returned her gaze to the fan. Look what they'd become. It was laughable, really. Two old friends with a sordid history, still unable to be honest about their feelings.

"I'm sorry, too." She was…and she wasn't. He deserved to be punched. Maybe not over pizza delivery, but certainly for dragging her here and making matters worse with the I-think-you're-beautiful admission. Still, punching him and fighting with him wasn't solving anything.

Alice let her eyes close.

"We'll figure this out. Technically, neither one of us has done anything wrong. Morgan cheated. She deserves the brunt of disdain. You and I will go home. I'll get the plant. You'll get your theatre. And we can forget about the rest."

The rest. Like this. Her stomach pitched. She wasn't sure she'd ever forget what it felt like to lie next to him in bed, the heat from his body warming her left side, the scent of him stirring fantasies in her head. Or how it felt when his breath tickled her ear. Or how he looked shirtless in the summer sun. *The rest* wasn't going to go quietly.

"Do you hear that?" His whisper shivered along her skin.

She prayed for him to quit talking. Then maybe she could forget he was there long enough to fall asleep and wake up ready to go home.

"Do you hear the ocean?"

In all the chaos of their argument, she'd missed the loud whooshing, pulsing noise permeating the glass sliding door.

He sighed. "I could lie here forever and listen to that sound."

God help her, because she could, too, and she hated the romantic notion, mostly because it was another impossible dream. Congressman Mitchell didn't have the freedom to stay here. Back home he had a mess to clean up. And in three weeks, when congressional recess was over, he'd be back to D.C., listening to the yapping of all the yes-men and women who followed him around, basking in his glow. Alice didn't want to bask in the glow of anything but her own accomplishments, and being here put her theatre behind schedule.

A list of construction projects left undone formed in her head. The rotting hardwood floors. The ripped cushioned seats. The lack of lighting. The need for sound. Foggy incoherent thoughts garbled the list, but when she stirred a moment later, the words inside her head were loud and clear: Nothing mattered but the theatre.

On an exhale, Alice released the remnants of tension preventing sleep. In the morning, she'd wake up ready to go, ready to make her theatre a success. And Congressman Mitchell could do whatever he damn well pleased—as long as he stayed away from her.

CHAPTER FIVE

So much for Congressman Mitchell keeping his distance. When Alice woke to darkness, his arm was behind her neck, his opposite hand on her waist, and she was thoroughly confused. The ocean thrashed beyond the sliding door. Mouse snored at the foot of the bed. Justin slept on the pillow beside her. Several seconds passed before she knew she wasn't dreaming.

On a shallow breath, she lifted her gaze to Justin's shadowy face, and tried to imagine how they got to this overly-friendly—entirely too comfortable—position. Maybe she tried to wake him again. Maybe he was the one who'd been dreaming.

Don't wake him now. If she could slip out of his arms and his bed, she could spend the rest of the night in the guest room, alone, pretending the whole world hadn't jumped its axis the moment she stood up in church.

Before she could make a move toward freedom, her stomach grumbled, echoing over other noises in the room. She held her breath and waited for Justin to stir. He only inhaled, lifting her body on the strength of his chest. She rode the wave, savoring the peaceful moment while studying his face. Moonlight peppered his cheek and sparked in his hair. The deep lines of worry that etched his forehead earlier had disappeared.

Alice's heart swelled, crowding her lungs, making it hard to breathe. This was dangerous.

She tore her gaze from his face and stared at the flash of stars outside the window. How did she get here? She closed her eyes and struggled with a shaky breath. It didn't matter how she got here. She *was* here, not here in North Carolina on his honeymoon where she didn't belong—that was bad enough—but *here* in his arms. If she were being honest, she'd have to admit she liked it here. She liked it, because she liked him. A lot. She breathed again, deeper this time, taking in his fresh scent and stoking her desire.

Now was a terrible time for honesty.

His arm tightened around her shoulder, fusing her to his side. She opened her mouth to breathe and swallowed a mouthful of him as her lips pressed against his chest from the force of his hug. Reflexively, she hugged him back. He felt good, strong. She'd never felt so safe.

His thumb strummed the curve of her bare shoulder, churning the emotion in her chest. She loved him. Still. She should leave. And she would have, if she'd ever been the kind of girl who did the sensible thing.

While she struggled with herself, he nuzzled his cheek against her forehead and flattened his palm on the curve of her waist. Her breasts heated against his rolling chest, and the sensation opened a pit in the lowest part of her stomach.

This was crazy. She was wrapped in Justin Mitchell's arms. One tip of her chin and her lips could touch his throat. The thought caused pleasant chills to trip along her body until she ached enough to test the limits of her sanity, tilting her face to his neck, setting her nose to his throat. But she stopped there. Even though the darkness dulled her inhibitions, the thought of her mouth on his body had her body scared stiff. Besides, any minute now he'd wake and stop the insanity.

She waited for reason.

Instead, he strummed the flesh at her waist, each swipe of his fingertips pushing her closer to the edge. With her heartbeat echoing in her ears, she breathed him in and out, one minute cursing her weakness, the next wondering if it would be so awful to steal one kiss. Probably. It would screw her up royally, that was for sure. But wasn't she already screwed?

His hand smoothed over the dip in her waist, back and forth, bunching her dress, until he rode the curve of her hip. She shuddered, surrendering to the ache in her core. Less than an inch, and her lips were on his throat, brushing over his Adam's apple, skimming the scratchy arch beneath his chin. She was definitely going to rot in hell, but what was an eternity of flame compared to the unbearable heat of this?

He gripped her hip and pulled her closer, close enough for her to feel his erection. Guilt over their predicament and the way she was taking advantage of him warred with the want burning her soul until she was too confused to care. *Screw it.* She'd always been a loose cannon where Justin Mitchell was concerned. Why should this time be different? Sure, this particular situation sucked extra hard, but wasn't the mass of SUCKINESS even more of a reason to get something pleasurable out of all the pain?

Yes. Yes it was.

And so she kissed him.

For the longest time, Alice's lips didn't move. They simply pressed against his as she breathed in his quickening exhales. But then he startled her by kissing back, opening his mouth and tangling his tongue with hers until she couldn't feel anything but her body freefalling into unbelievable bliss.

Too bad he was sleeping. Too bad he'd wake soon. Too bad…

His hand skimmed the outline of her body until it found her breast.

Alice sucked quick breaths when he slowed the kiss to suck on her bottom lip. Was he awake? She started to open one eye, but thought better of it, mostly because his thumb was strumming her tightened nipple through the cover of her clothing, and she'd be damned if she did anything to come between that hand and her breast. She squeezed her eyes shut and savored.

Slipping her tongue over his lips, she rocked her pelvis against him, and when he groaned, she smiled. He had to be awake. She hoped he was awake. The idea that he might not know who was giving him pleasure cooled her off a bit, but the reprieve from the heat didn't last long. He wrapped his fingers in her hair and pulled hard enough to wake every nerve ending, raining pricks of pleasure all the way to her toes.

More kisses. More desperate gropes. Her dress bunched around her waist. Her panties slanted across her hips. Surely he was awake now. She should say something. Make sure. She moaned instead.

Justin said nothing in return, did nothing to make her think he was any more or less aware than he was a moment ago. With one hand beneath her dress and inside her bra, he continued to tweak and tease, coaxing rapid breaths. With the other hand, he gripped her head, positioning her for kiss after soul-melting kiss.

If he wasn't awake, he was one hell of a sleeper.

Did it matter? No. Alice was going to do this. After years of dreaming about it, she was going to have sex with Justin Mitchell, because girls like her rarely lived their fantasies. She molded herself to him, while distant waves crashed against the shore. Tomorrow she'd worry. But not now, not when Justin's tongue traced the outline of her lips. Tonight she'd enjoy.

• • •

Justin was going to do this. He was going to roll over and drive into Alice so hard and deep he'd rid himself of the demon of desire that had hounded him for years. He'd have regrets. Absolutely. But it was hard to care with her hand smoothing over his zipper. No, the question wasn't whether or not he was going to do this. The question was, Alice on bottom or Alice on top?

He grunted, pushing her flat on her back, the decision made by the head in his pants. In this position, he could cover her, causing friction in all the right places while he conquered her mouth with his tongue. There wasn't going to be any nicey-nice foreplay, not after they'd been teasing each other for ten torturous years.

She shoved hands beneath his shirt and dug fingernails into his flesh.

Hell, yeah. This was going to be explosive.

He kissed her harder, holding on to the back of her neck. His other hand reached for the bedside table where condoms littered the drawer. She sucked the skin at the base of his neck and traced the tip of her tongue along his collarbone. Every inch of his overheated body wanted this, wanted her.

He dragged his hand past the alarm clock, over the edge of the table and reached for the handle, but before he could open the drawer a vibration stopped him cold. The sound of thrumming against the wood overshadowed their heavy breathing.

His phone was ringing.

Damn. If he opened his eyes…if he faced what he was about to do…if he looked at Alice or the Caller ID…he was screwed, and not in the way he wanted to be.

She froze beneath him, no doubt listening to the horrible buzzing too. Her lips stilled against his neck. Her hands stuck to his lower back.

Reality seeped into his carnally consumed brain, and reality was pissed. Justin clenched his teeth. What had he been thinking, carrying on with Alice like this? He'd already left a mess at home. Why make a mess at the beach? This call amounted to divine intervention. With a huff, he slid off Alice and looked at his phone. *Will.*

Justin let the call go to voicemail despite a surge of panic. Of course, he was panicked. He was going to sleep with Alice Cramer. But as the seconds dragged on, Justin's chest constricted until it was almost impossible to breath.

Something else was wrong—something big.

• • •

Alice refused to wear Morgan's dress home, and Justin refused to waste time shopping. She showed up in town, wearing the same dress she'd worn the day of the wedding. Only now, the dress was brittle from salty ocean air and too much sun, and her skin screamed for something clean and soft. She dragged the dog across the front lawn by his collar as the traitorous animal whined for Justin.

"Stop that," Alice hissed, glancing over her shoulder at the cloud of dust trailing Justin's Audi down the dirt road. She was home. She wanted to be home. She thought she'd feel better than this.

The grass needed cut. The grass had needed to be cut before she left. As she tugged Mouse away from a weathered chew toy, she reminded herself that she'd only been gone for two days. But she felt ten years older, tired. Her muscles misfired, shaking whenever she gave them a command. Her heart aged the most. It hurt to breathe. *Damn Justin.*

Clouds loomed overhead. Alice stumbled onto the porch and shoved Mouse through the ripped screen door. Eleven hours spent side by side with Justin in a moving car, and she still wasn't any clearer about what had happened between them at the beach. In that bed. He hadn't said a word about it. His focus was on his ailing mother.

Alice assessed her depressing surroundings, which somehow seemed more depressing than usual. The house was a wreck. It had always been a wreck. Why did she expect something different? She bent down and picked a ratty throw pillow off the floor, tossing it on a faded couch. Crows cawed from their perch atop the backyard shed. Mouse barked in reply. He raced from the room, disappeared into the kitchen, and a moment later she heard him scratching the back door. At least someone was happy to be home.

She'd be happy, too…as soon as she *was* home. At her theatre.

Alice walked into the kitchen to free Mouse from the house. As she walked, she bent her arm behind her, forcing her hand over the scratchy bodice of her dress until she reached the prone-to-stick zipper. She tugged. It barely budged. The dog whined. She switched hands, opening the door with her right while she tugged the zipper with her left. The dog released; the zipper didn't. She growled. Mouse barked. The crows flew away.

Alice faced the dingy kitchen and spied Mama's sewing shears in a rusted coffee can. She stopped fussing with the zipper and snatched up the scissors, cutting the left dress strap in a spot where she was certain repair was possible, and then she cut the right strap just the same. With an arm across the bodice to stay covered and the scissors still in hand, she left the kitchen and passed through the hall, where Charlie showed his face.

Alice jumped, her heart in her throat, her hand mere seconds from wielding the dull weapon.

He craned more of his body around the doorjamb of his bedroom, a sneer marring his face. "Look what the cat dragged in."

He was dirty. His greasy hair clumped, and a pathetic beard shadowed his face. But he was sober. His flat eyes were clear. The usual bittersweet emotions of seeing him safe after an extended disappearance gripped her heart.

"You're home." She sounded like an idiot, stating the obvious.

"Yeah. So are you."

Not yet. But as soon as she was dressed she'd be headed there.

"Was that Justin's car? I thought you were with Kory."

Alice expected the questions, tried to prepare for them on the ride home. She hoped to avoid details and keep things vague. Besides, she had a few questions of her own. "Charlie…it's complicated."

"I'm sure."

"Margaret had a heart attack."

"I know." Two shadows slashed the already harsh, bony terrain of his face. He bowed his head.

Charlie wasn't a bad guy. He made bad decisions. The booze was to blame. When he was sober, he had moments of shame and concern like Alice. But like Mama, he was too weak to get out of a bad situation. Alice was stronger, except when it came to Justin.

"You slept with Morgan."

"I know that, too." He shrugged. "Justin's too good for her."

Alice's throat shut, leaving too much blood in her head where it could burn her face. Public opinion was that Justin was too good for most people, especially people like her. She walked passed Charlie and headed for her bedroom.

"He's not too good for you."

She stopped inches from her door.

"But that doesn't mean he's right for you. Don't be stupid, Alice."

She winced. "I don't know what you're talking about."

Closing her bedroom door behind her, Alice returned to hacking the dress, cutting it at the seams. A tear fell for every cut, not only because she regretted the damage to the fabric, but because despite Charlie's words, she knew the truth. The beaten dress slipped from her hips and gathered at her bare feet.

An arm's length away, an empty bottle of whiskey littered the matted-shag floor. At the beach. In the dark. In that bed. She thought it possible for a man like Justin to love a woman like her. At home. In this family. In this skin. She knew she'd never been so wrong.

It wasn't new information. It wouldn't lead her to despair. She was just so damn tired of the reminder.

CHAPTER SIX

Justin stomped the gas pedal, fishtailing the Audi around another bend. Dirt gathered in the rearview mirror and clung to the trunk of the speeding car like the devil breathing down his neck. A few more miles and he'd be in the clear, back on paved roads, far enough away from Alice's side of town to not look guilty.

But he was guilty.

The steering wheel vibrated from the blow of his fist. How could things have spiraled so out of control?

Scenes from the church flashed in his head, and he ground his teeth to dull their impact. He hated what happened there, the drama, the speculation, the stress that no doubt led to his mother's heart attack. But as much as he hated the mess and his mistakes made on display, he couldn't imagine not walking away. What was the alternative? Marrying a liar and a cheat wasn't worth a thousand plastics plants. Nope. No changes there.

But the beach was a different story.

He growled and pounded his foot on the brake pedal milliseconds before he blew through the only stop sign on this side of town. Yeah, he'd change a thing or two about the beach. For starters, he wouldn't have gone. He would've stayed in town, consoled his mother, and taken care of business. Instead, he dragged Alice to the beach and …

Memories flickering in his head heated his face. He told himself to think of something else. His mother. The plastics plant. His reelection. Anything but Alice. He'd driven eleven hours without acknowledging what happened in that bed. He'd be damned if he gave it credence now. Bottom line, the longer he went without acknowledging it, the closer he'd be to forgetting it.

Justin hit the gas again, spewing gravel in his wake, taking his eyes off the road for a moment to watch the plume of dirt in the mirror. When he looked forward again, he saw the one car he didn't want to see. Morgan's car sped past. There was no mistaking the vehicle; there was only one convertible Jaguar in Harmony Falls. And there was no mistaking Morgan's destination; the road behind him dead-ended fifty feet from Alice's house. He gripped the wheel, torn between the need to turn around and manage the confrontation and the need to move ahead and see his mother.

Morgan turned around instead. Justin watched her pull a donut in the middle of the dirt road. She closed the gap between them in a matter of seconds. The closer her car got to his car, the tighter his hands wrapped around the wheel and the harder the muscles in his face clenched. More than once, his right foot twitched on a fleeting thought to slam the brakes. But at this speed, on these roads, someone would get hurt. Not that they weren't already damaged.

His cell phone rumbled in the cup holder beside him, and he glanced at the caller ID. Of course she'd call to demand he stop. Too bad for her he wasn't going to answer. Looking in the rearview mirror, he saw her glaring, one hand on the wheel, the other gripping her phone. Nope. He wasn't going to answer, and he wasn't going to stop. If she wanted to talk to him, she was going to have to follow him. Not to the hospital. No, he wanted to avoid another scene. He would lead her to his house, lure her away from Alice, and say his piece in private.

It seemed like a reasonable plan, but one block into town, Morgan turned right and disappeared. Panic pricked a path along his skin, and he locked his jaw, stifling the urge to turn around and follow her. He had to get a grip on this propensity to panic. The uncontrolled emotion led him to do stupid things. His mother needed to be his top concern. Like it or not, whatever was going to happen at the Cramer house was going to happen without him.

His throat squeezed and his swallow turned painful against the blockage. Could he trust Alice to not make things worse? She had barely talked to him on the way home, preferring to sleep—or feign sleep. What words they did say were stilted and utilitarian. "Can you stop at the next rest area?" "I need gas." "Mouse has to pee."

With a hand clammy from strangling the steering wheel, he lifted his cell phone and dialed Alice. The call went straight to voicemail.

"Morgan may be headed your way," he ground out after the beep. "Leave. Avoid the confrontation as long as possible, at least until we can go over what you should say." *Stop telling me what to do,* she warned in his head. But how could he when there was so much at stake? The Parrishes were powerful people. One wrong move, one wrong word …

Pulling into the hospital parking lot, Justin dropped his phone into the cup holder and refocused. What may or may not be happening at Alice's house was bad, but what was happening in this hospital was worse.

•••

Morgan Parrish's over-waxed Jaguar idled in Alice's driveway while Charlie sat on the front porch steps, arms drawn tight across his chest. From a split in the living room curtains, Alice could see Morgan on the phone. Who was she talking to? The police. Fat chance they'd drive out to remove Charlie from his rightful spot on the porch so Morgan could get to Alice. Better chance she was calling her daddy. That man would stop at nothing where his daughter was concerned.

Alice wrinkled her nose and swallowed the foulest tasting spit. How was she going to get out of this one?

She glanced at her phone, sticking between tattered edges of couch cushions. *Leave. Avoid the confrontation.* Justin was a jerk. He got her into this mess and the best he could do to get her out was advising her to leave until he figured out what she should say? Alice squeezed the keys in her hand and growled. Morgan was blocking her car. Now what, genius?

Between being trapped and being told what to do, Alice snapped. She wasn't going to be a prisoner in her own home, and she wasn't going to let Justin put words in her mouth. She'd been standing up for herself too long.

Peeking between the curtains again, she watched an intimidating Morgan cross the lawn. True, Alice didn't want to face the banshee any more than she wanted to face what happened between her and Justin in that bed, but she was used to not getting what she wanted.

Sometimes low expectations were an advantage.

Alice dropped the curtain from her hand and stalked toward the screen door.

"We need to talk."

Morgan's voice made Alice falter two steps from the door.

"I got nothing to say. Go on. Get." Charlie talked to her like he talked to the dog.

Alice smiled and took another step.

"Don't be that way. Charlie, look at me."

What the heck? Alice froze again, close enough to the screen that she held her breath for fear of being heard. Why was Morgan's tone so familiar, pleading, even?

"Charlie, I'm pregnant."

Alice gasped, and the tail end of the gasp turned to a squeak—a loud squeak.

"Was that the dog?" Morgan asked.

Alice wished, but it wasn't. It was her, and the rock-hard ball in her gut told her she'd overheard something Morgan didn't want her to hear.

"Mouse," Morgan called, but Alice knew the mutt was long gone, making up for lost time, chasing crows.

There was a shuffle and the sound of hard-soled shoes on the porch. "Is it Alice? Son of a…Alice, are you in there?"

"Morgan, go." Rustling mixed with Charlie's voice, and then Alice saw Morgan's hand wrap around the screen doorknob.

The jig was up. With her hands to her heart, Alice closed her eyes and readied to face the banshee.

"Go," Charlie roared, and when he did, Alice opened her eyes to see Morgan's hand had disappeared from the door.

A few thuds, and then quiet. Was Charlie carrying Morgan off the porch? Was she struggling as he dragged her to her car? What the hell was going on? Alice leaned ever-so-slightly forward for a glimpse out the screen door.

"Alice," Morgan screamed.

The couple wasn't off the porch. Morgan stood with hands on Charlie's waist, while Charlie's hands were wrapped around her upper arms. Intense? Yes. But intimate, too. Alice's eyes widened.

"Don't come out here," Charlie warned.

Alice inhaled and rolled her shoulders back, stepping into full view. "Don't tell me what to do."

When she walked onto the porch, Charlie let go of Morgan and spun on Alice, stomping a cowboy boot against the rotting wood. "Damn it. Go back inside. You're going to make things worse." He grabbed her shoulder and shoved.

The pressure of his fingers stung, and Alice thought to fight back, but then she saw Morgan, eyes wet, lip quivering. Good God, she was pregnant? But by whom?

Alice opened her mouth to catch some air.

"No." Morgan poked a shaky finger around Charlie at Alice. "You do not get to speak. You said enough in that church, and believe me, I'd be strangling you right now if…"—she smoothed the same hand across an oversized silver belt buckle and then down the front of her pencil-slim skirt—"…I thought it would solve anything."

"Is it mine?" Charlie released Alice and tipped his head, rolling his eyes to the peeling porch ceiling. A muscle in his cheek twitched.

Or is it Justin's? Alice's stomach flipped. She wasn't sure which answer was worse. If it was Charlie's, there went the Cramers screwing up things again. If it was Justin's…Alice held a hand to her mouth. The idea of Justin having a baby with anyone but her …

Morgan stood ramrod straight, glaring at Charlie's back. Not a muscle moved in her body until a large lump appeared at her throat. Alice watched the knot slide down until it disappeared beneath the crisp collar of Morgan's blouse. "I'm not having this conversation in front of her."

"Fine. Then we won't have this conversation." Charlie lifted his head and reached for the screen doorknob.

"Charlie, stop." The panic in Morgan's voice revved Alice's heart rate and thickened her confusion. "Of course, it's yours." Morgan winced.

Of course? Alice whimpered. Charlie was going to be a father.

He turned to face Morgan, nodding once. Twice. Alice couldn't see his face, but she could imagine his shock. "Are you going to kill it?"

Morgan gasped. "No. How could you even…" And then all her lawyerly composure fled her face. Nostrils flared. Eyes bulged. And a wail left her lips. She flung at him, driving fists into his chest. "Why, Charlie? Why? Why did this have to happen?"

Alice pushed off the wall and tried to wedge between them. "Stop it."

What the hell was happening?

"Get off me." Morgan took a swipe at Alice's face, scratching her jaw, causing a burn beneath her skin. "You shouldn't be here. You…" Morgan swiped again.

Charlie shoved Alice out of the way and wrapped an arm around Morgan's waist, hauling her off the porch. "Calm the hell down."

Alice backed into the house for balance. There was so much—too much—struggling for space in her head. Charlie and Morgan weren't a drunken one-night stand? Justin would be devastated. Morgan was pregnant with Charlie's baby. The Parrishes would be mortified. Broken engagements and cheating were bad enough, but babies out of wedlock with the "wrong kind of folk" caused an even bigger scandal for politically minded people.

At least Justin was free. He'd never take Morgan back after this.

Alice balked at the stupid, random thoughts. Justin might be free, but he wasn't free for her. He'd never been. Despite what happened in that bed. Especially after what happened in that bed. Especially after this. Alice was Charlie's sister. How could Justin look at her and not be reminded of everything the Cramers ruined?

"I cannot raise a baby fathered by a Cramer. My father would disown me."

Alice flinched. True as the words were, they stung.

Charlie threw up his hands, shook his head. "Yeah. He'd take away that fancy car for sure. Maybe buy you something used instead. Hell, something American." He fake-shuddered. "That's hardship, I tell ya."

Alice cringed at the sadness in his voice. She wanted to comfort him. She wanted to tear Morgan apart. She wanted somebody, anybody to explain what the hell was going on.

Morgan shook her fists. "You don't understand, Charlie. You never did. There are expectations. And this…"—she jabbed at her belly—"…is not one of them."

Alice thought about slinking away. She probably could have. At the moment, Morgan was in some sort of emotional trance, ignoring Alice as she begged for Charlie's understanding. It was surreal.

"I'm so confused," Alice stuttered.

"Oh my God." Morgan slapped her palms to her forehead. "Why are you still here? This doesn't concern you. Leave." She balled her fists again. "Charlie, listen to me. Come with me so we can talk."

"Save your breath," he said, climbing the stairs at a slow and heavy pace.

"No, I need to say this now so you'll understand later… when…"

"Do what you have to do."

"I will. I…I'm going back to Connecticut tomorrow, where I'm going to find a family to adopt it." Her voice shook, and when she laid a hand on her belly, Alice felt a sting in her heart. Charlie must've heard the waver, too, because he stopped walking. But he didn't turn to face her. "Neither one of us can sign away rights until after the birth and a requisite number of days have passed. It's not long, just a few days. You're going to have to sign, Charlie. We can do it by mail, but you're going to have to sign. End of story. No fight. Not a word."

Charlie walked into the house, slamming the screen door behind him.

Morgan hung her head and wrung her hands. For a minute, Alice wanted to hug her—she looked that broken—but then she lifted her chin, sighed and sort of snickered. She was the spitting image of her snooty mother. "You Cramers really know how to mess things up."

Alice didn't blink. "Funny, I was thinking the same thing about you."

Morgan narrowed her eyes and after a few long strides, stepped onto the porch. Any semblance of the emotional wreck she'd been disappeared in anticipation of the confrontation. "If you think for a minute you can run off and open your mouth about this, think again. Charlie loves me. He would love this baby. One rumble from you, and I'll be forced into an abortion." She blinked too much, too fast, and her brows dipped to touch above her nose. Again she clutched her belly. "That would kill Charlie." Her lips twisted as she nodded. "And it would be your fault."

How dare she garner sympathy and threaten all in one breath? Anger sat heavy on Alice's chest until she opened her mouth and sucked enough air to shatter the weight into digestible pieces. "Get off my porch." Alice stepped forward, backing Morgan down the stairs to the grass. "And get off my lawn."

"Gladly." Morgan was already stomping to her car. But when she threw the door open, she stopped, drew an exaggerated breath and stared at Alice. "You know, you can't have Justin. He's going to be president. He and my father have plans, big plans, and they don't include you. Can you imagine? Justin cavorting with the town joke? You're a community college graduate who happens to be the sister of his childhood friend, the friend who knocked up his fiancée." Her laugh sounded unhinged. "It's a circus, Alice. You've caused him and this town nothing but trouble. Leave him alone."

Alice stood on the porch long after Morgan drove away. The world outside was as topsy-turvy as her insides, and she couldn't see a way to set things straight. If she walked inside the house, Charlie would be waiting, and if he hadn't started drinking to dull the pain, she doubted he'd be willing to talk, to explain, to help her make sense out of what had happened. So Alice stepped off the porch and wandered over the grass to her car, which was parked with one bald tire crushing the bachelor buttons in Mama's weed-wrought garden.

If she could get to her theatre without any more drama, she could pretend to be someone else, someone happy, someone who had a shot at her dreams.

• • •

Justin walked into the hospital lobby with his nerves steeled. He hadn't been beyond the bronze dedication plaque, bearing his family name, since the day his father died. He avoided the sights and sounds of sickness at all cost, preferring to send elaborate flower arrangements in his place. When that didn't work, an assistant or two delivered Congressman Mitchell's words of encouragement. Neither impersonal gesture would work today, so he held his breath until the elevator doors closed behind him.

Alone with his discomfort, he raised his palm to his nose and breathed in the scent of his skin. It was better than the antiseptic cleaners that tried to block the smell of death. That smell remained in the lining of his nose for months after his father died.

For the hundredth time he checked his phone screen. And for the hundredth time he scolded himself. Alice wasn't going to call, no matter what was or wasn't happening at her house. She was on her own. She liked it that way. And he needed to stop trying to control what he had no business controlling in the first place.

The doors opened. Justin set his face, rolled his shoulders and powered his strides with shallow breaths. He shivered. Mostly because it was cold, but partly for other reasons he didn't wish to analyze.

"Justin."

Robert Parrish's voice hit Justin like a smack to the base of the skull.

Justin sucked a quick breath for fortification. He didn't want to face the fallout from his actions at the church here and now. He needed to see his mother, but slighting the man who paved Justin's way to a congressional bid wasn't an option. Without Robert's money and backing, without his original plan, Justin would be… what? The question wedged into his brain with enough force to cause an instant headache.

Despite the pain, Justin conjured a neutral expression and turned to see Kitty Parrish walking away. Her heels slapped the linoleum floor like it was Justin's face.

Robert sniffed. "Morgan is moving back to Connecticut. Kitty blames you…and that ridiculous Cramer girl, of course." He looked around the empty halls and then stepped closer to Justin. "I, however, am a bit more…forgiving."

Looking at the sneer on the face of the man Justin considered a mentor, he didn't see any forgiveness. He saw cold, hard ambition, and a man who was willing to make serious concessions to accomplish his goals. Why hadn't he seen that before?

Robert dropped a hand to Justin's shoulder and squeezed. "Whatever happened between you and my daughter is over. She's going quietly." He drew a breath through his mouth, and the ensuing crackle of saliva turned Justin's stomach. "I can't ask for much more than that…except for proof of your commitment. You strayed from the plan, son, and I don't like surprises. There are going to be some changes, starting with you on a shorter leash. I expect your complete cooperation."

A shadow caught Justin's eye, and Robert smiled extra bright, extra slimy, when a nurse passed.

"Good afternoon, Mayor Parrish."

"Carly," Robert said, bobbing his head in acknowledgement of her greeting. "I was just telling Justin that his mother is one lucky woman. Isn't she?"

"Yes, sir." Carly beamed, continuing down the hall.

Robert slapped Justin's upper arm. "Very good then. Go take care of your mother, and I'll go find my wife."

Not until Robert disappeared around the corner did Justin realize he hadn't said a word. Robert dominated the conversation. Maybe he always had. This time, rather than cordial plotting and planning, he tossed barbs and—if Justin's powers of perception weren't mistaken—threatened with words like "shorter leash" and "complete cooperation." Those things didn't rest peacefully on Justin's already troubled mind. In fact, they felt downright ominous. He'd given complete cooperation to every part of the plan—until he walked out of the church. Complete cooperation almost tethered him to a liar and a cheat. What would complete cooperation get him now? And while it was only natural for a father to question the commitment of the man who walked away from marrying his daughter, under the circumstances was it necessary to threaten with a shorter leash? Justin never failed to deliver when it mattered most. He understood the plan…the congressional seat…the plant…the presidency. He and Robert wanted the same thing, harmony in Harmony Falls.

Justin dropped his chin to chest and squeezed his temples. What was he doing standing in the hallway like this with campaign slogans running through his head? Why was he thinking about political agendas when his mother was down the hall recovering from a heart attack? *Priorities*.

And Robert had the audacity to question his commitment.

"Hey."

Justin lifted his head and turned toward the voice.

Will, cell phone in hand, strode toward him. "End of the hall. Hang a right. She's fading fast, so hurry."

Justin's heart slammed against the wall of his chest. "What?"

"Sorry. Bad choice of words. She's tired, drifting off, going to sleep. Take your pick." He raised his phone to his ear and gave Justin's back a pat. "I'll only be a minute."

Walking the remainder of the sterile hallway, Justin's heart rate retained its scattered beat. His mother's tiredness was expected, but hospitals were containers for the unexpected. One minute his father had been smiling and squeezing his hand, the next minute he had been coding.

Not the same, Justin thought, rubbing his fingers across the tight skin of his forehead. Cancer obliterated his father. His mother suffered a heart attack. His brain knew the difference, but his throbbing heart and burning eyes proved his body didn't.

He wished Will would return. Will was the rational Mitchell brother. He'd keep things focused when Mark started accusing Justin of breaking his mother's heart. But maybe Justin deserved the blame. After all, he walked out of that church knowing full well his actions would jeopardize the decades-long relationship between the Mitchells and Parrishes.

A foot from the door, Justin paused and looked behind him for Will. The hall was empty. So much for moral support. He pressed a palm over his nose and mouth, and took one last deep breath. All too soon he was dropping his hand, setting his face, rolling his shoulders and stepping into the room.

"You look like hell." His mother propped on pillows, while Mark sprawled in a chair beside her bed. She was pale, like the sickly green of the hospital gown gaping around her bony neck, and she was angry. He could tell by the hitch in her withered lips and the flare of a single nostril.

Angry or not, she was alive.

Justin crossed the room to the slow beeping of the monitors which were attached to every inch of his mother. At her side, he kicked Mark's leg out of the way and leaned over to place a kiss on her clammy cheek. "I'm sorry I wasn't here," he whispered. He would've grabbed her hand, but the sight of the IV pooling with drops of her blood was enough to make him woozy.

When he straightened, her shoulders slumped and her gasp echoed, sounding an alarm of beeps.

Mark shoved Justin aside to grab her hand. "It's okay, Mom."

Justin looked at the call button, resting beside his mother's IV-tethered hand. He took a step away from the bed, ready to run for a nurse.

Mark fawned over her like he had since the day their father died. The more he stroked her thinning hair and spoke soothing words, the more the beeping slowed.

But Justin's heart rate didn't. It wasn't that he believed her to be in grave danger. He'd seen his father sicker than this. It wasn't that he wanted to comfort her. Mark had a solid hold on that. Justin's racing heart was likely the byproduct of the panic that had been his constant companion since the church, a feeling that he was careening out of control.

Mark sat back and glared at Justin. Words weren't needed to convey his message. Justin knew Mark blamed him for the heart attack. Nothing new. Mark blamed Justin for everything. Justin used to think it was the result of jealousy. After all, Mark's token role in the family business was more a result of genetics than professional prowess—it was hard to make a name for yourself when you were busy gossiping with your mother. But now, along with the panic, Justin was feeling paranoid. Maybe Mark's resentment was warranted.

Justin chewed his bottom lip and watched his mother struggle for sleep. The scattered thoughts, beeping machines and chill temperature of the room, made him just as restless.

"You're going to look back one day and realize none of it was worth it." Mark said, adjusting in the creaking vinyl chair.

"Easy for you to say," Justin retorted without taking his eyes off his mother. "You only have one person depending on you. I have thousands."

Mark scoffed. "You're a self-crowned hero, bro. And that's the worst kind."

"Gentleman, another time, another place." Will strolled into the room. "I have news. Robert and Harold want to meet."

Justin snapped his head to attention. "When?" *Finally.* Now they could get the plan back on track and forget about the misstep at the church.

"In a half hour."

The monitors' beeping accelerated, drawing Justin's attention back to his mother. "But I just got here. I haven't spent any time with her."

"They asked to meet with Mark and me…without you."

Justin twisted his neck, causing a muscle strain. "Hell, no. I spearheaded this deal. I'm going to close it."

"You nearly destroyed it," Mark said, standing.

For a man who showed little interest in business, Mark was certainly enthusiastic to be included in the meeting. The funny thing was, despite his vibrato, a part of Justin was more than happy to miss the powwow and spend time with his mother. The sad thing was, he was too much of a control freak to bow out gracefully. "I'm going."

"No, you aren't." Will shook his head. "Robert said he'd see you bright and early tomorrow morning in your office instead… something about keeping you focused on the campaign."

Mark rolled his eyes.

"I can focus on MCI *and* my political career. I *am* focused on MCI and my political career. This is crazy." The panic consumed him, clawing its way from the pit of his stomach and burning a trail across his face.

"Maybe." Will said. "But I think it's wise we cooperate with them until we know where this plant deal is headed."

Complete cooperation.

Justin winced. This was his deal, his mess. He should be the one fixing it. He was always the one fixing things. But for the first time in years, he'd lost the vote of confidence.

Even worse, he didn't have a plan to get it back.

CHAPTER SEVEN

Alice opened the cupboard doors in the box office and screamed. A dead mouse—at least she thought it was dead—littered the middle shelf. She slammed the door and ran into the lobby, shaking her head and hands, jumping from one foot to the other, hoping to wiggle the disgusting image out of her head.

"Yuck. Yuck. Yuck."

Now what? After years of watching her mother cower under the thumb of a man, Alice prided herself on not needing one. But there were times when one would come in handy. She covered her face with her hands and growled in frustration. No, *she* was going to handle the mouse.

Bolstered by a few deep breaths, she tiptoed to the office doorway and peeked inside. What if he wasn't dead? What if when she opened the cupboard he jumped at her? She whimpered and held a hand around her neck, sealing the gaps in her T-shirt collar. *Oh God.* This was going to be a nightmare.

She stepped inside the office and listened. If he scurried, so would she. She stepped closer still, the only sound the echo of her open-mouth breaths. She could leave him there, couldn't she? She didn't have to do this. There were so many other things to do. Stacks of boxes lined the second-floor rooms. She could sort through those. But what if there were mice in the boxes, too?

With another squeal, she retreated to the lobby, shaking her head. She needed an exterminator. She needed a cleaning crew. She needed…the grant. Maybe then she'd get some help, because right now, she was a little overwhelmed with the mouse, the theatre, Charlie. She couldn't believe he was going to be a father. She couldn't believe she was going to be an aunt. She couldn't believe neither one of them would ever hold that baby.

Alice slumped into a folding chair.

"Hi." The greeting sounded simultaneously with the scraping of the front door. Justin stepped off the darkened street and into the lobby. "I was coming from the hospital and saw the lights on." He shoved his hands into his pants pockets and hitched his shoulders to his ears. "How'd it go with Morgan?"

Alice stifled a miserable laugh. Justin didn't want to know. Oh, he thought he did, but looking at his wrinkled forehead, red-rimmed eyes, tousled hair and crinkled clothes, she knew he was under enough stress.

"How's your mother?" Alice asked instead.

"She's going to be okay."

"Are you going to be okay?"

He scoffed. "Of course."

She raised her brows in an I-don't-believe-you sort of way.

"It's just going to take some time," he continued. "How much time all depends." He pushed a breath past flabby lips.

"On what?"

"A lot of things." He shuffled his feet, drawing Alice's attention to his loafers. They seemed to have lost their shine. "Did Morgan find you, or did you leave before she got there?"

"She found me."

Justin sighed. "I told you to leave." His voice was missing its usual strength.

"And I told you to stop telling me what to do." Maybe the exhaustion from the long drive and Morgan's admission and the mouse in the cupboard had tempered Alice's mood, because there wasn't an ounce of anger in her words. In fact, she smiled, hoping to settle him and absolve her of any guilt that would come with avoiding the whole truth about Charlie and Morgan. "Relax, Justin. I didn't say a word about the beach. I barely said anything."

"What'd she say?"

A lot. Too much. So little that was safe to repeat. Alice gulped and latched onto the least painful truth. "She said…I can't have you." It still hurt like hell.

As an awkward silence filled the lobby, memories of the one and only time she'd almost had him filled her head. The air crackled between them.

Damn him. Damn the beach. Damn whatever stupid feelings lingered.

Wrinkles from his forehead dropped to the bridge of his nose. "Alice, I…"

"Can you get rid of a mouse for me?" It seemed like a safer subject.

"Excuse me?"

"There's a dead mouse in my office. I'd like him gone."

Justin sucked a noisy breath through his mouth and nodded. "Yeah. Sure."

Thankful to be free of the two topics she wanted most to avoid, Alice stood and walked to the office. "It's in there," she said, pointing to the cupboards.

When he passed, he brushed a hand over the small of her back. It may have been an innocent gesture meant to gain him space to slip into the room, but that thought didn't stop heat from searing her shirt and scalding her skin.

He looked around the room. "Do you have something for me to grab it with? A plastic grocery bag, maybe?"

He hadn't shaved since the wedding. She'd noticed it in the car while they were racing away from the beach. The stubble she'd grazed with her lips had darkened, giving him a dangerous edge. It was dangerous because he didn't look at all like Congressman Mitchell.

She stared a little too long.

"Alice, a bag?"

She startled. "Yes. No. I mean…" Looking around the messy room, she expected to find a grocery bag. "You'd think so, huh? What about some rags? I think it's dead."

His green eyes widened and blinked. "You think?"

"I don't know. He didn't move when I screamed, but I didn't keep the door open long, so I didn't get a good look."

With his shoulders rising and falling, he shook his head. "Is it in a trap?"

"I don't think so."

Still shaking his head, he opened the cupboard door. "It's dead."

"Good."

He walked to a nearby pile of garbage and grabbed a pizza box. A petrified piece of pepperoni pizza slid onto the floor, landing inches from his shoes. He looked at the pizza and then at her. "No wonder you have mice." There was a touch of Congressman Mitchell in his sneer.

Alice snorted in defense. "I have mice because the theatre is old and empty."

"You need to clean this place before it's condemned," he warned.

She glared at Congressman Mitchell as he walked out of her office, carrying the box in both hands. He probably deserved a thank-you, but she hated the fact that he was still telling her what to do, so she bit her tongue and waited for the front door to scrape. When she heard it, she exhaled. With the mouse gone, she could get back to work.

Moving to the pile of trash where Justin found the pizza box, Alice cringed. It was a mess, but it wasn't solely hers. Some of the trash, like the empty cartons of cigarettes, came with the building. Regardless, she needed to clean, but not because Justin told her to.

With a grunt, she dragged an empty box toward a pile of garbage and shoveled some trash inside. It was a gross job, but somebody had to do it. Since she didn't have help—yet—the only somebody around was her. And if cleaning up kept the mice at bay, she'd do it.

Alice picked up an empty soda can and drilled it into the side of the box. Next, she reached for some water-stained paper towels.

"Start a separate box for non-recyclables."

She jumped, and turned to see Justin, pulling a box to the pile beside her. The cuffs of his shirt were rolled up over his forearms. "What are you doing?"

He bent at the waist and gathered ancient magazines. "I'm helping you." He tossed the tattered papers into his box and bent again to grab a dried-out paintbrush. "Slide your box closer."

"Why?"

"So I can reach."

The box was on her right, but she didn't move. "No. Why are you helping me? I cause you nothing but trouble, remember?"

He straightened and tilted his head, his jaw pulsing. "I don't want to argue, Alice. I want to stay busy, do something constructive."

"I thought you said your mother was okay."

"She is."

"Then…"

"I don't want to talk. I want to work."

"Fine." Alice pitched another can into the box.

The more they cleaned, the more she questioned his motivation. He came for answers about her confrontation with Morgan. He got those answers—as far as he knew. Why was he still here? What could he be avoiding that was worth the risk of being here with her?

"How long are you planning to stay?" she asked out of frustration.

"Until we get this room clean, and then…"

"No 'and then.' You should go, Justin. This is…awkward. You don't want to be here anymore than I want you to be here."

He shook his head. "This theatre will be good for the town. As your congressman, I'm obligated to do what I can to help."

She rolled her eyes. "Leave, Justin. I wouldn't want to damage your precious reputation with a questionable association. I can clean up by myself."

But he didn't go. Those damn dusty loafers stuck in her view. She reached past him for a crinkled sub wrapper.

"Alice…"

"Go away."

He huffed and puffed above her, finally shuffling his feet. "I'm sorry about what happened at the beach. It was inappropriate."

Her face flushed, and shame rose like bile into her throat as she leaped to stand. "Ha," she yelled in his face. "I'm not sorry." Shock at the explosive admission forced a gasp from her lips, but her tirade continued. "You can be sorry, but I wanted that for so many years—too many. In case you haven't noticed, I don't often get what I want, so I'll take it." She shoved him. "I'll take what I can get."

His emerald eyes sparked as his brows climbed his forehead. He looked tired and unhinged, and she could only imagine what he was thinking. Whatever it was, it was probably remarkably similar to her thoughts. She was an idiot with a big mouth.

"I'm sorry. I…"

Alice rolled her eyes and shook her head. "Stop apologizing. I get it. I do. I've ruined everything. I'm a screw-up. You look at me and all you see is one giant regret."

When he squeezed his eyes shut, she knew it was true.

• • •

Justin couldn't look at Alice as long as her bottom lip quivered and her eyes filled with tears. She didn't deserve to be dragged into the vortex of his breakdown. He should go home, where he could brood and self-implode in private.

He opened his eyes with every intention of leaving.

"Alice…" He touched his fingers to her lifted chin and pressed his thumb to her lip, wanting to stop the trembling. Her breath hitched, and he didn't see a trace of this so-called regret. He saw passion, strength…and breathtaking beauty.

Something raw and rowdy socked him in the gut and twisted his insides until he dropped his hand to her wrist and pulled her in. She squealed as she careened into his chest, but a moment later there was silence when his mouth covered hers. He wanted to make her forget the bad. He needed to forget a few things too. Warped logic? Maybe. But months of strategic planning hadn't saved him from ending up here, so why not give in?

He parted her lips with his tongue and heated when she softened, her little hums and moans lulling the worry from his mind. Like the purest drug, the high came swift and hard, leaving no room for regrets. Alice made him forget.

His hands roved the soft skin on her back while her hands grasped his biceps. "No regrets," he whispered against her lips.

She whimpered, and the sound had him sliding his hands over the curves of her bottom, readying to lift her into his arm when …

"Alice," a man's voice called from the lobby.

She broke from Justin's arms, pushing against his chest and stumbling backward until she bumped a filing cabinet. "Charlie," she whispered, lip quivering, eyes wide. And then she bolted from the box office.

Justin stood reeling from the kiss, cursing the reality that brought Charlie here to remind him of what a mess his life had become—a mess he needed to clean up. Those were his choices: stand and brood or face Charlie, say his peace and put some space between him and the chaos-inducing Cramers.

Justin always was a man of action.

By the time he stepped into the lobby, Alice was pushing Charlie out the front door.

"Let him stay. He owes me an apology." Justin tensed his muscles, hoping it was enough to hold his body in place and keep his fist from Charlie's face.

Charlie scoffed overtop Alice's head. "What's *he* doing here?"

Good question, and the answer was getting murkier all the time. What *was* he doing here? His lips still burned from the kiss, adding to his sense of disorder. He hadn't come for that kiss. That was yet another mistake.

Damn it. Justin wanted to get a grip. But with anger bubbling his blood, he knew he wasn't going to be getting a grip on anything but Charlie's collar.

"Did you think for a minute when you were screwing her that she was someone else's fiancée?" he asked.

Alice kept her head down and her hands against Charlie's biceps while she tried in vain to shove him onto the dark street. Charlie smirked as he pushed her away.

"Did you think for a minute when you asked her to marry you that she was in love with someone else?"

Yeah, Justin thought about it, but there wasn't room for sentimentalities when there was power and progress to gain...or so he'd told himself. And now, here he was, wifeless and powerless while his brothers holed up with Harold and Robert Parrish, making decisions without him. Still, he was better off than the mess of a man who was stalking across the lobby toward him.

"Face it, Charlie. You needed more than love to claim Morgan Parrish. You needed a job...and a new last name."

"Get out." Alice rocketed past Charlie to Justin, poking a finger to his chest. "You will not insult *my* family on *my* property." She backed up against Charlie, raising her arms at her sides, blocking his path to Justin.

The rage in her eyes drilled a hole in Justin's heart. He'd meant to humiliate Charlie. He dragged Alice into the fray…again. When was he going to stop behaving like a lunatic? When was he going to leave her alone, so they could go back to the way things used to be? Separate. Peaceful.

"I'm sorry," he said.

When she lifted her chin and closed her eyes in haughty refusal, he surrendered his need to make things right. It was probably better this way. A little anger between them would help him keep his distance.

Dodging her outstretched arm, he left the theatre without another word. No apology from Charlie like Justin expected.

These days, nothing was what he expected.

CHAPTER EIGHT

Emotion warred in Alice's chest, making it hard to breathe. She was as breathless with anger at Justin's insult as she had been breathless at his kiss. He made her stark raving mad, but right now Charlie's mental state was her bigger concern.

He'd never come to her theatre before. She hadn't seen him since Morgan broke the news. And God only knew the last time he'd seen Justin.

She faced him. "I didn't know he was coming. I didn't know you were coming." Threading fingers into her hair, she tugged at the roots. "I need to start locking that door."

Charlie stared at the space above her head, looking vacant. She half expected his words to slur. She fully expected his anger.

He opened his mouth and sucked a deep breath. "I want to be a father to that baby," he said in a whoosh. There wasn't a slur to be heard. Then he dropped his face to his hands and sobbed. For his baby.

It shredded Alice's heart.

"I love her. I do." He lifted his head, and it was as if he flipped a switch. The tears disappeared, leaving the anger she expected in their place. "She loves me too, damn it. It's this town, the games. These freaking people are insane. He's crazy too." Charlie punched a finger at the door where minutes ago Justin had been. "And they're screwing with us, ruining our lives. Don't you see it?" He shook his head "I do, and I won't let them do it anymore. Not to me. Not to her. Not to you."

Alice had seen him angry before, but this was different. Without alcohol as fuel, he was eerily lucid and strong enough to make good on his vague threat. She placed a hand on her chest to steady her breathing. "Charlie, if you tell people about the baby, you'll make things worse. Robert will strong-arm her into…"

He crossed his arms over his chest. "He'll have to strong-arm me first. I'm going to Connecticut…and I want you to come with me." He stepped closer and rested his hands on her shoulders. "Let's get out of here, away from all their games. We can start over, be whoever we want to be."

Be something other than Cramers. That's what he really meant.

An oscillating fan buzzed in the distance, and cooled the sweat spot between her shoulder blades. When the grant came through, she planned to repair the central air conditioning. She doubted even an industrial-sized condenser could banish this kind of heat.

"I can't," she said, shaking her head and blinking back tears.

"Because of him?" Charlie sneered, giving her shoulders a shake. "He's not capable of loving you, Alice."

"No," she cried, hoping the louder she talked, the deeper she'd bury the voice in her head that wanted just that. Justin. To love her. She swatted Charlie's hands from her shoulders. "This has nothing to do with him." Her throat convulsed. "I don't want to start over someplace new. I want to finish here. Finish this." She looked around the ratty room. Good God, she had so far to go.

Charlie shoved his hands into his jean pockets and looked around the room too. He probably saw the same hopeless dream she did.

"Suit yourself," he said, hitching his lip in the same show of disapproval he used to give Mama when she chose their father over a better life. But when he looked around the room again, his face softened. "If anyone can make this happen, you can."

Alice threw her arms around his neck and buried her face in his shoulder. "Promise me you'll be okay. Promise me."

"I promise." His lackluster pat on the back wasn't much assurance, but it would have to do. He was already unlatching her arms and backing toward the door. "I'll call you when I get there." And then he disappeared, like Justin had, into the darkness.

She closed the door, twisted the lock and struggled to warm herself against the chill of loneliness. Charlie had never been the best brother, but he was her only brother. When he pulled out of Harmony Falls, she'd be the last Cramer standing. Suddenly that felt like a very scary thing to be.

•••

After the tumultuous evening, Justin couldn't sleep. Rather than toss and turn, worrying about his behavior and what was or wasn't happening in the meeting, he went to work before sunrise. Three hours and two pots of coffee later, he couldn't think straight, so he stared out his office window across Main Street at a platinum blonde, climbing a ladder in flip flops. She was going to hurt herself.

Reaching over her head with a rag in hand, Alice swiped at the yellowed marquis. One foot slipped off the rung, and she wobbled, grabbing the sides of the ladder with both hands.

He clenched his fists and resisted the urge to walk over there and demand she get down. *Stay away, Justin.* He had no business telling her what to do. Besides, Will was on his way, bringing details from last night's marathon meeting and a contract bearing Harold Parrish's name.

Alice stumbled again.

Justin slapped his palms against the radiator and groaned.

"Forget to put money in the meter?"

Will appeared in the doorway. "He got me last week for fifteen bucks. I tried to give him the damn quarter right there, but he refused. Bastard." He tossed a cocky smile as he strolled to Justin's desk and dropped a folder. "Signed, sealed and delivered."

It stung to think he was receiving the details of the meeting secondhand, but Justin did his best to check the bitterness. "Did you have to give up your firstborn?"

Will laughed. "Like there'd ever be one of those to give."

"Did he undervalue the property?"

"He tried."

"Did he ask us to finance?"

"He did."

"And?"

"Robert refused."

Justin puzzled. "You agreed to finance a thirty-acre land transaction and Robert refused?"

"Yep. Something about the Parrishes not needing to be indebted to the Mitchells." Will shrugged. "Doesn't matter. It's better for us. We get the lump sum for the land rather than payments."

Justin nodded, agreeing with his brother's financial assessment, but a sense of foreboding lingered. Then again, maybe the sleeplessness skewed his response.

"I need to run. I have a nine o'clock with Carson to discuss union sanctions at the mill." He was already moving toward the door. "Look it over and let me know if you have questions."

Which was pointless. Questions could lead to changes, and it was too late for that. Justin picked up the contract and flipped the pages. Besides, what questions could he possibly have? This was a basic sale of land. The incentives he'd worked so hard to put in place would be levied by local government—Robert Parrish and his board of merry men.

All that power Justin thought he had? Turned out, he had none.

With a sigh, he glanced up from the contract, catching sight of Alice again. She had a broom by the bottommost part of the handle as she stretched her body to reach the furthest corner of the marquis. She was inches from falling—hard—but he was powerless to help her too. And she needed help. She needed someone with the proper equipment to make that theatre operational again. But to hire someone, she needed the grant.

Justin surged with purpose. Maybe he wasn't powerless after all.

By the time Senator Kathleen Boyd took Justin's call, he'd made a mental list of the work facing Alice. In his rough estimate, the sixty grand the grant offered would be barely enough to repair the façade she was risking her life to clean.

"I'm calling on behalf of Alice Cramer." Even though his office door was closed, Justin lowered his voice around her name.

"Encourage her to apply next year," Kathleen said.

Disappointment furrowed Justin's brow. "So she didn't get it?"

"You know I can't reveal results until the winner has been notified, but as your friend and colleague, I'm telling you to encourage her to apply next year. You can interpret that however you'd like."

Justin gnawed his bottom lip. There was only one way to interpret it. "And there's nothing I can say or do to change your mind."

Kathleen chuckled. "There are ten minds on the committee, Justin, and they've all been made. Let me say that the winner is impressive…and a repeat applicant. Like I said, encourage her to apply again next year."

He stifled a groan. Without immediate help, Alice would be in full traction by next year.

"Thank you, Kathleen. I'll let her know."

It wasn't a conversation Justin was looking forward to. Not after last night and the way he'd behaved. First the kiss, then the insult.

He hung up the phone and rested his forehead in his hands. Maybe he wouldn't tell her. She'd get the official news soon enough. Why insert himself where he didn't belong? Why keep concocting reasons to see her?

"Congressman Mitchell, Mayor Parrish is here."

Justin nodded toward the bodiless voice, coming from his desk phone. "Send him in."

Another conversation he wasn't looking forward to …

"Mitchell." Robert walked into the room with his shoulders squared and his head back. "You have a few weeks of congressional recess left. I think it's high time we form a political action committee. Test your broad range appeal. Raise some dough." His gaze locked like radar on the contract.

Justin expected acknowledgement of the meeting he'd been unceremoniously excluded from, but once again his expectations were wrong. Robert returned his gaze to Justin, and continued to ramble about precursors to a presidential bid.

All the while, Justin's ornery mind churned, ruminating on the last several hours. He hadn't just been blocked from a pet project, he'd been excluded from MCI business. MCI. Mitchell Company, Inc., the company that bore his name.

Screw being powerless.

"Robert…" Justin held up his hand, halting the blowhard's soliloquy. "…how does forming a PAC lead to my exclusion from last night's meeting?"

Robert sniffed and stared out the window. His eyebrow raised, and Justin wondered what he saw. Then he remembered Alice.

"You need to focus on what's most important, Mitchell. If you lose focus, you lose elections." He turned his head and glared at Justin. "I did you a favor, son. This is small potatoes compared to where you're going." He tapped his sausage-like fingers atop the contract.

Justin slapped his hand on the uppermost edge of the same document, causing a twitch in Robert's shoulders. "*This* is my family's company. There never has been, nor will there ever be, anything small about it. I did this…"—he gestured around his congressional office space—"…for my father and the future of MCI."

Robert's lips pursed in a skeptical sort of way. He looked out the window again. Seconds of silence ticked by. "Do you think she knows it's a lost cause?"

Justin flinched. He might be ready to speak loud and clear for himself, but was he ready to do the same for Alice?

Robert chuckled. "She'll make out in the end. Selling that shithole to Harold will bring her enough dough to bankroll another venture, maybe a strip club. She sure has the ass for one, just as long as it's not around here."

The voice Justin didn't think he had pushed past the lump in his throat and exploded out his mouth. "Excuse me? What the hell are you talking about?"

Robert rolled his beady eyes in Justin's direction. "Oh, that's right. You missed the meeting." He tapped the contract again and clucked his tongue. "Page thirteen, an ironic number since it's one hell of a lucky deal—for everyone."

Justin refused to be goaded. Robert had warned him there'd be a test. Perhaps this was it. If so, Justin wanted to pass…so he could figure out what was going on and bring about its end.

With an imperceptible breath, Justin nodded. "I haven't had the chance to read through the contract yet." Which was the point, wasn't it? If Justin was a betting man, he'd put money on Robert excluding him from the meeting for this very reason, a reason that had to do with Alice selling her theatre.

"Don't bother," Robert said with a twisted smile. "It's boring as hell."

Yeah, Justin bet it was. Still, as soon as he was rid of Robert he was going to flip to page thirteen, and then he was going to read the contract from front to back, and then read it again. He had news for the Parrishes. No matter what this document said,

Alice wasn't going to sell. She had big dreams and big plans for the theatre.

He just wished she had the grant to get her there.

Robert walked toward the door. "We'll talk, Mitchell."

You bet we will, Justin thought as he reached for the contract. He had the document opened to page thirteen before the carpet cooled from Robert's feet. Justin skimmed until he read:

The sum of three hundred fifty thousand dollars ($350,000) as payment in full for land and buildings located at one hundred ninety-eight (198) Main Street and two hundred two (202) Main Street.

Harold bought more than thirty acres of land on the edge of town for his plastics plant. He bought the vacant buildings on either side of Alice's theatre too. If she agreed to sell, he'd own the block across the street from Justin's congressional offices. But why would Harold want to? Thirty acres of land was more than enough space to house the plant and its corporate offices. Unless those thirty acres weren't high profile enough for what the Parrishes had planned.

A dull ache at the base of Justin's skull had him squirming. Whatever the scheme, Alice wouldn't sell. But without the grant, she'd think about it. He couldn't let her take them seriously. If she sold, they might as well rename this town Parrish Falls. Maybe that was what they wanted. Talk about power.

Justin tossed the contract aside and returned to his earlier spot by the window. What would his father think of the sacred plan now that it had mutated into a means to control other people? And if Justin's hunch was right, the Parrishes wouldn't be happy until they had complete control at the highest level.

Bracing his palms on the radiator, Justin hung his head. *Harmony in Harmony Falls* had been his father's campaign slogan. Marvin dreamed of joy and prosperity in the town he loved for generations to come, and there'd been harmony—when Justin towed the line, much like his father had. But there was nothing harmonious about Justin's exclusion from last night's meeting or the hurtful gleam in Robert's eye when he talked about ridding the town of Alice Cramer.

Justin lifted his head and stared across Main Street. He had a choice to make: a false sense of harmony or a fight for what was right.

Alice and her ladder were long gone, but the yellowed marquis remained. He tried to imagine the streetscape without it—without her. He couldn't. And he wouldn't let that happen. The disappointment of losing the grant and the daunting task of rehabilitating the theatre might tempt her to sell, to give up on her dream, but she had options. He'd just make damn sure she knew what those options were.

So much for keeping his distance.

CHAPTER NINE

Alice stared at her monthly direct deposit slip from the energy company. Receiving four hundred dollars a month as compensation for unused Cramer land to house wind turbines had seemed like a generous gift when she and Charlie first signed on the dotted line. But after she bought the theatre, not a day went by when she didn't wish they'd negotiated for more. Not that she was ungrateful. The initial lump sum paid by the company to replace transmission cords across the property was what allowed the theatre purchase in the first place.

Four hundred dollars. Alice sighed. She needed groceries, gas for her car, and there were utilities to pay. Thank God Charlie used his portion of the lump sum to pay off the mortgage.

But what about her theatre? She needed bulbs for the fixtures in at least one hallway, a back staircase and the alleyway door. Tossing the piece of paper on the kitchen counter, Alice marched into the living room, straight for Mama's reading lamp. Nobody had turned it on in years. She unscrewed the dusty bulb. So what if nobody could turn it on now? Nobody was here anyway. She was always at the theatre, and Charlie was gone.

He said he'd call when he got to Connecticut. He should've been there by now. She pushed away her worry and dropped the bulb in her coat pocket, setting out in search of more.

Alice looked around the room, but hesitated to take anything too useful. The bulbs would have to come from unused spaces, like Mama and Daddy's room. There, she stole the bedside bulbs.

Kinda like robbing Peter to pay Paul, she heard Mama say. The pitiful truth made Alice laugh.

With her pockets full, Alice fed and watered Mouse, and then returned to her theatre. She kept her cell phone on the passenger seat in case Charlie called. Why hadn't she heard from him?

Driving down Main Street, she noticed the bright glow of Justin's office light. Congress was in recess, but still the congressman worked late, putting his stamp of approval on those who were worthy. She wrinkled her face, grinding her teeth, wanting to march into that office and give him a piece of her mind. He had known Charlie loved Morgan and he went through with the proposal anyway. What kind of friend did something like that?

She was no expert on friendship, having preferred imaginary friends to judgmental live ones. Only the awkward girl down the street, the one who operated on squirrels and birds who'd been shot with BBs by the hooligan neighbor boys, found a way into Alice's life. Kory and Alice never would've so much as looked at the same guy. Then again, Kory and Alice weren't wrapped up in any so-called political games. Maybe Charlie was right. Maybe the Mitchells and Parrishes were crazy.

Alice glanced at Justin's side of the street again. "Keep your crazy over there," she said with a sassy grin and pulled around the block to the alley. But even as she said it, she knew she didn't mean it. As much as Justin's recent actions hurt her, she wanted to understand him more than she wanted him to stay away. Love made a person want the craziest things. Huh, maybe she was crazy too.

Shaking her head to scatter thoughts of Justin, she inched the car between dumpsters and crumbling brick walls. She wished somebody would get enough courage to buy the empty buildings beside hers, fix them up and make their entrepreneurial dreams come true. Then maybe she wouldn't be the only one driving in and out of this creepy alley.

Something scurried in front of her slow-moving car, and she shuddered. Having more people around was bound to cut down on the rodent population.

Parking so her headlights illuminated the backstage door, Alice got out of the car and snatched a bulb from her pocket. A couple minutes later, she stepped back and smiled at the soft glow of security light alongside the backdoor. *Thanks, Mama.*

Something rustled in the dark distance, and Alice snapped her head in the sound's direction, struggling to see beyond the blinding headlights. Her heart pounded.

Harmony Falls is safe, she thought. Nothing remotely dangerous ever happened here, unless one counted crashing the congressman's wedding. She swallowed a whimper, certain her overactive imagination was to blame. Imagination or not, if she had money to waste, she'd open the backstage door and bolt inside, leaving her car to run. But that half-tank of gas needed to last her until next month's direct deposit.

Walk to the car, Alice. Walk to the car. Turn off the engine. Get inside the theatre. Nothing's going to happen. There's nothing after you.

She sucked a breath and stepped toward the car.

Good girl.

She took another step. And another. And another. Until she reached her open door and leaned inside, snatching her cell phone off the passenger seat and the keys from the ignition. When she did, the headlights darkened, and the alley shadows lengthened.

Wind kicked up around her, scattering old newspapers and other debris. *The wind of change*, she thought for some odd reason. She rolled her eyes and slammed the car door, shuddering against the chill. It was just a storm moving in. Nothing ominous about it.

Three leaps, and she was back in the glow of the security light, her heart throbbing in her throat. Adrenaline skittered beneath her skin as though someone was watching her. But who?

Before she could answer her silly question, someone screeched.

Alice lunged for the door, grasping the handle at the same time a black ball of fluff sprinted over her feet. More screeching, and a gray ball of fluff darted past. Two kittens collided, rolling around in the dim light showering her feet.

Their cuteness calmed her fear, and Alice crouched beside them. "You guys scared me."

She glanced around the alley for more. Litters were usually bigger than two, but then again, life on the street was hard. Maybe only two survived.

The wind howled again, and the kittens scurried away, disappearing behind the dumpster closest to her theatre. It wasn't much of a shelter, not with a storm moving in. If she could grab them, she'd take them inside until the storm passed. They'd stay dry, and she'd have company.

Alice snatched an empty cardboard box off the stack she'd disposed of earlier in the day. With a little luck and much less aggravation than she expected, she wrestled both kittens into the box and closed the flaps. They mewed and clawed at the cardboard.

"It's all right. You'll be fine," she said as the wind whipped the hood of her jacket around her throat.

Once inside, she locked the backstage door, flipped the light switches and chatted to the whiny kittens as she carried them across the stage, down the stage-left stairs and through the dimly lit house. Only when she arrived in the relative safety of her office—with the door closed—did she let them out.

The black one hissed.

"Well, that's a fine thank-you."

The gray one bolted across the room, hiding behind a box Alice was using as a trash can. So much for company.

She returned her attention to the black kitten hissing at her feet. "I'm going to call you Oscar, partly because this is a theatre, and Oscar Hammerstein wrote amazing songs. But mostly I'm calling you Oscar because you're a grouch." She hissed back at him. Or her. She wasn't sure.

Alice reached into her pockets for her cell phone and the remaining light bulbs. She walked over to the desk and lodged the light bulbs between a stack of old playbills she'd found upstairs and her foam container from lunch. *Lunch.*

"I bet you guys are hungry." She opened the lid and pulled turkey from her leftover sandwich.

Grabbing a paper towel from the roll, Alice cleaned a spot on the floor and tore the meat into cat-sized pieces. Oscar ate.

As she sat and watched the black kitten chow down, the gray kitten emerged. "Hey, you," Alice whispered, not wanting to scare him off. "You better hurry up before Oscar eats it all."

He made it in the nick of time.

Oscar grazed Alice's knee as she watched the gray one eat. "So we're friends now, huh?" She chuckled. "I see how you are. You must be a man. Feed you, and you're sweet as pie."

The gray one finished the turkey. "And you…you're Rodgers by default. I can't have an Oscar Hammerstein without a Richard Rodgers. Welcome to my theatre, Rodgers and Hammerstein."

Alice smiled. It would be nice having somebody to talk to while she worked. Better yet, maybe they could chase away the rodents.

Strains of *Climb Every Mountain* echoed through the box office, causing Alice to jump to her feet. *Charlie*, she thought before she saw the caller ID.

She was right.

"Hello."

"I'm here." He sounded tired—and very far away.

Alice wrapped her free arm around her waist and hugged. "Have you seen her?"

"She won't take my calls."

Alice had been afraid of that.

"But I'm going to keep trying," he said, yawning. "What else can I do?"

"Where are you going to stay, Charlie?"

"I'll sleep in my car, save my money for gas."

God, she knew the feeling. Only she had a house and a bed. "Let me send you some money."

"No," he snapped. "This is my battle, Alice. Keep focused on that theatre."

She was trying to, but it was getting harder all the time.

• • •

Justin ducked his head and charged into the wind, heading across the street to the theatre. He'd put this conversation off long enough. Truth be told, he would've kept procrastinating if he hadn't seen her lights come on. But now that he knew she was in there, he needed to relay the bad news so they could figure out what to do next.

He pushed against the door. It didn't budge. Damn it. Since when did she lock her door? *Probably right after you left the last time, buddy.*

He knocked. The wind swirled around him as sprays of icy water chilled his cheeks. He knocked again. At this rate, he might get his wish to procrastinate awhile longer. If she didn't answer soon, he'd be forced to leave.

This time he pounded.

The door cracked open.

Alice glared at him through narrowed eyes. "No soliciting."

"Who says I've come to solicit you?"

Her face reddened. He wasn't even through the door and already the air heated between them.

Justin resisted the urge to pull her to him and warm his soul. "Can I come in?"

She wrinkled her nose. "Why?"

"It's wet."

She lowered her lid over one eye, looking unmoved.

"And I have news." He hated the direct approach.

"News about what?" Batting thick lashes over those baby blues, she looked him over from wet head to soaking loafers.

"The grant," he ground out, wishing she wasn't making him work so hard for entrance.

At the mention of the grant, she couldn't move aside fast enough.

When he was safely inside, she locked the door behind him. Too bad she hadn't taken the same care last time. Then they wouldn't have been so rudely interrupted.

Justin forced a hand through his wet hair. Why was he thinking about last time? Last time could not happen this time. He was here to help her, not to seduce her.

"What about the grant?" she asked, punctuating the question with the perfect pout.

With his attention on her lips, he couldn't stop thinking about their kiss. The ill-timed thought frustrated him.

"It's bad news. I can tell by the look on your face." Her shoulders slumped. "Just say it, Justin."

"I'm sorry…" He started to apologize for his distracted behavior.

"I didn't get the grant, did I?"

He shook his head. "No, you didn't."

She took a deep breath through her open mouth, widening her eyes as her lungs lifted with air, and then she huffed an exhale. "It figures." She sucked another breath, even longer this time. When she exhaled, she looked smaller. "How do you know?"

"I called on your behalf."

"To make up for insulting my family the last time you were here?"

"Partly." It was the other part he dreaded the most.

"And there's nothing I can do? It's a final decision?"

"I'm afraid so. For what it's worth, Kathleen did encourage you to apply again next year."

Alice's laugh was hollow. When the mirthless sound quieted, another sound took its place. Scratching.

"What's that?" Justin asked, looking over his shoulder toward the sound.

Alice sighed. "More mouths to feed." And then she passed him, walking to the box office door where she turned the knob and unleashed two scrawny kittens. "I found them in the alley."

Justin stared at the balls of matted fur. It was just like Alice to be rescuing kittens when she couldn't even rescue herself.

She bent to pull one away from a rotted floorboard. "I'll have to keep my eye on them when they're out of the office. It's not exactly safe around here." The dejection in her voice relayed what they both knew—without the grant, it wasn't going to get better anytime soon.

The gray kitten scurried towards a loose wall vent.

"Grab him, will you?" she asked, her hands full of one squirmy kitten. "I don't want him getting lost in the wall."

Justin snatched the kitten out of harm's way. Two bright blue eyes peeked at him through a puff of gray fur. "He's cute."

"Exactly. That's how they ended up in here." She was standing beside him, clutching the black cat to her chest, massaging the tiny space between his ears with her fingertips. And she was smiling— even after the news about the grant.

"How do you do it?" Justin whispered, letting his gaze wander over her beautiful face.

"Do what?"

"How do you keep smiling even when things go wrong?"

She shrugged. "There's always going to be bad news, especially when you're a Cramer." Her smile faltered. "I learned a long time ago to take my smiles wherever and whenever I could."

And that made his attack on the Cramer name even worse. Self-disgust bubbled in his throat, and he knew her forgiveness was the only antidote. "I'm sorry I insulted your family."

She blinked. "Don't worry about it. I'm used to it."

"But you shouldn't be. And you shouldn't be judged for what your father did or what your brother is doing."

A flash of fear danced across her face, widening her eyes and halting her breath. "What's my brother doing?"

Justin blinked this time. "I just meant the drinking, the carrying on with…"

She tipped her head and scoffed. "It's my understanding that Charlie and Morgan love each other, and you tried to come between that. Do I get to judge you for that?" She shifted the black kitten into the crook of her left arm and then slipped her right hand beneath the kitten in Justin's arms. "I'll put them back."

Justin didn't make the transfer easy. He held on a second too long, making her move closer and shove her hand deeper. "Go ahead and judge me, just know you'll never judge me half as harshly as I've been judging myself these last few days." Silence, dark and deep, swirled around them, tying them together until neither one of them moved. "Everything's changed, Alice. Everything."

She didn't look at him. It was probably a good thing. If she raised her face to his, he was going to kiss her to wipe away her judgment and to prove the changes, and he shouldn't—for lots of reasons, the biggest of which was the fact that he hadn't told her about the Parrish threat to her theatre.

Justin released the kitten, and Alice stepped away. "There's more news," he said, deciding it was best to nip the wayward feelings in the bud with a good dose of reality.

Her face littered with lines as she nodded and scurried off to close the kittens into their room. When she returned, the lines remained, and her hands busied with wringing. "What?"

Justin crossed to her and raised a hand to smooth her upper arm. "Harold Parrish wants to buy your theatre."

She raised a brow. "Why would Harold want to own a theatre?"

"It's not about the theatre. He wants the land. He already purchased the property on either side of you."

She shook her head as she brushed his hand from her arm. "My theatre's not for sale."

Justin smiled. "I'm glad to hear you say that."

"Was there ever any question?"

"A little."

She rolled her eyes. "Then you don't know me very well."

They were innocent words, but somehow they presented a challenge. Her eyes sparkling, staring, waiting didn't lessen the pressure he felt.

"I know you, Alice," he said, tightening the gap between them until he could feel her body's heat. "I know that as soon as I leave, you'll sit with this news and stare at these walls and wonder what you're going to do without the grant. I know that despite that smile, you carry a gut load of worry. I know you go home alone, where you miss your mother and pray for Charlie—and fall asleep clinging to your dreams."

She closed her eyes and a tear rode the curve of her cheek. He swiped at it with his thumb. Yeah, he knew her pretty damn well, so well he couldn't get her out from underneath his skin. So he did the only thing he could do.

He kissed her, sliding his lips across her wet cheek to her mouth, where she breathed through parted lips, tickling his tongue with her exhale.

Her hands came to rest on his chest beneath his suit coat. "We're going to keep doing this until we really mess things up, aren't we?" she asked, nipping his bottom lip.

"Yes, we are…unless you want me to stop." He wound his arms around her waist, pulling her closer. "Should I stop?"

"No."

So he didn't. And he wasn't going to this time. With the front door locked and his phone in his car, he couldn't imagine what could interfere. With her body pressed against his, he didn't care.

She edged up on tiptoes, tightening her arms around his neck. "All I want is you. All I've ever wanted was you."

There was power in those words. They rocketed through him like a lightning strike, charging every cell. He dropped his hands to her bottom and lifted her to his waist, kissing the breath from both of them as she grasped him with her legs. He backed them into a wall, grinding against her, feeling her mouth on his neck, her fingernails on his back.

More kisses. A groan. He dragged her shirt over her back to feel her hot skin. But when she sunk her teeth into his earlobe and chased away the sting with a swirl of her tongue, his knees buckled.

"Put me down. You're going to get hurt."

He pressed his body against hers and silenced her self-deprecation. Somewhere between the unsteady knees and the mind-blowing mixture of tongues, she ended up with feet flat on the floor, her hands shoved into the waistband of his dress pants.

She was right, wasn't she? Life was full of lots of crap. Why not seize every smile?

CHAPTER TEN

Alice wrapped her hands around Justin's belt buckle and tugged, pulling him toward the far side of the room. Of course there wasn't a bed in the theatre—not even a blanket. There was no couch either. No padded armchair. And since the grant was a bust, it looked like the building would remain empty for a long, long time.

Good thing she knew how to improvise.

Even better, she had years of practice shedding the skin of poor downtrodden Alice. It was easy really—take on the persona of someone else, someone without a care in the world. Usually that someone else was a singing nun or a sweet, simple farm girl. Tonight, she was channeling Gypsy Rose Lee.

And that was going to get her something she'd always wanted—Justin—without disappointment over the grant getting in her way.

A deep breath and a shake of her head, and she let Alice Cramer go. As a nameless, fearless woman, she pulled a devastatingly handsome man through the theatre's double doors. Once inside the dimly lit house, he backed her against the wall and stole another kiss, piling goose pimples on top of goose pimples. When he came up for air, she shook the tingles from her head and dragged him down the center aisle.

"Sit," she commanded, twisting him around until the front row was at his rear.

He didn't hesitate. What man would? She was already unbuttoning her shirt.

"Welcome to the show." She winked.

He pulled on his tie as he cleared his throat.

She grinned and unbuttoned another button. "You're in for a treat." So was she. There was no way she'd squander another opportunity where Justin was concerned.

He reached for her wrist, but she jerked away, giving her hips a sassy swing. "Keep your hands to yourself, sir. No unauthorized touching in my club." She released the bottom button and slipped the shirt off one shoulder, careful not to show too much skin.

Running the fingers of her opposite hand down the curve of her neck, she bared a few more inches.

His eyes grew dark.

She loved the power he was letting her have. She loved the want written all over his face. And she was just getting started.

"Sometimes when I'm alone, I imagine you touching me here," she said as she dragged fingers over her collarbone to the split in her shirt, creating a deep V. "And here." Then she flattened her palm and pulled it across her breast. "And here."

He released a good-natured growl. "Alice, you're killing me."

She flashed him a sultry pout. "My name's not Alice."

"Of course not. Who are you?"

"Whoever you want me to be," she said, dipping her body to the floor, rolling her hips while she gripped the shirt to her chest.

"I want you to be Alice, and I want you over here." His voice went rough.

"Is that so?" She stepped closer, but then backed away as she rocked to imaginary music and dropped the shirt to the crooks of her arms. She hooked a finger beneath her bra strap and slipped it over her shoulder. "But if I come over there, you'll miss the show."

He groaned. "This is not going to end well?"

She pushed the other strap off her other shoulder and turned her back to him. "Why not?"

"I don't have a condom."

A few swings, and her capris slung low on her hips. "What a shame." With a single finger hooked around the belt loop, she sent them sliding to the floor.

"Tell me about it."

Ditching her sandals in a pile of denim, she turned and stepped toward him. "We can do other things." The tails of her plaid shirt covered her lacy bikini bottoms. She knew better than to give an eager audience too much too soon.

He grinned as she sashayed toward him. "I can think of a few other things."

"I bet you can." She grabbed his shoulders and straddled his thighs, liking his rapid inhale. "I always thought the first live performance in my theatre would be Sondheim or Schwartz, not striptease."

Justin clamped his hands around her waist. "I prefer this."

"Hands off," she said, swatting at him. When he grasped the armrests, she ditched her shirt.

His eyes widened and his breaths grew quicker still. "You always were a tease."

She lowered her body to his lap, sitting squarely on his hardest point. "I'm sorry. I thought men liked that." She rocked against him, bringing her hands behind her head, carrying the ends of her hair with them.

He dropped his head to the seatback behind him and groaned. "I can always stop…teasing."

"No." He grabbed her waist again, grinding her against him. When she shot him a nasty look, he let go.

"Good boy." She leaned forward, brushing her covered breasts against his chest, feeling her nipples tighten. "You can't touch me, but I can touch you," she whispered in his ear, licking his lobe. "I love a good double standard."

She had every intention of sitting back and grinding him crazy, but as she sucked his lobe into her mouth, rubbed her chest against his and rolled her hips, the heat between her legs threatened to boil her alive.

"On second thought, you can touch me now." She didn't have to ask twice.

Justin yanked the cups of her bra over her breasts and bent his head, drawing her nipple into his mouth. He teased one breast with his tongue and the other with his hand.

She gripped his head, holding him to her heart. She was breaking every rule she'd ever made where Justin Mitchell was concerned, and she didn't care. How could she when she was finally, torturously, witnessing a dream come true?

Tossing her head back, Alice moaned and ground her aching core against his erection. Shards of pleasure ripped through her breasts, pricking every inch of skin. She wished he had a condom. She wished she was on the pill. She wished …

For that. Justin slipped a hand inside her panties and rubbed the wet between her legs.

Alice whimpered, and with his open mouth over hers, he swallowed the sound. Pawing at his restricting clothes, she managed to loosen his tie and unbutton his dress shirt. But damn it if he wasn't wearing an undershirt.

Her frustration grew. What she wouldn't give to strip him bare, take him whole, share all his secrets.

He slipped a finger inside of her while he circled her sex with his thumb. *So good.* She rimmed his mouth with her tongue and buried her hands in his hair, finally giving in, knowing she was going to have to finish alone in order to have any chance at him.

Again he dipped his head, planting open-mouthed kisses along her neck to her chest, until he latched onto her nipple, driving her out of her body with a lick, a suck, a flick, a twirl.

The orgasm consumed her, like loving Justin always had.

• • •

Justin drew Alice to his chest, cradling her against him as she took one shaky breath after another. She pressed her lips to his neck, below his ear and sucked tiny kisses, kisses so small they shouldn't have mattered. But they did. They rocked his soul. Like Alice did. Every look. Every touch. She reached places no one else could.

It had always been that way.

"Your turn," she said in a voice more breath than sound.

Maybe it made him half a man, but he was content to stay like this awhile longer, so he held her there, on this lap, with his face in her velvet, vanilla-scented hair.

Time slowed. Seconds felt like hours. He reveled in the closeness, but then she tugged on his T-shirt, sliding it free of his waistband. The flutter of cotton against the skin below his navel tightened his erection. And when she slid back, balancing on the edge of his knees, working his belt buckle, giving him a front-row view of her glorious breasts, he was more than ready to move on to the next act.

Justin slipped his hands over her warm sides and reached around her back to unfasten her bra. He dropped the lace to the floor as Alice freed him from his pants. He had just enough time to brush her nipples hard again before she dropped to her knees between his thighs.

He'd dreamed of this, seeing Alice's blond hair spilled across his lap, feeling her tongue at his tip. A jolt of pleasure shot through him when she swallowed him whole.

He gripped the armrests, watching her head bob, savoring the hot, wet pressure. Another groan and he wound his fingers through her hair, guiding her movement, teetering on a loss of control.

She looked at him, just a glance, and something in her eyes annihilated him.

Justin surrendered, but she stayed at his feet until the pulsing stopped. And when she climbed into his lap again and wrapped her arms around his neck, everything really had changed.

He didn't want to keep his distance. He couldn't after that. In all the upheaval, she was the only thing that was real and constant. She didn't manipulate him. She didn't make demands. She wanted him, not for what he could do *for her*, but for what he could do *to her*. He could handle that.

She curled against his chest, like his very own kitten of comfort. "Now what?" she purred.

They should do it again. In a bed. With a condom. And… Justin was getting ahead of himself. Maybe that wasn't the sort of answer she was looking for. They'd never talked about what happened in the bed at the beach, or the kiss in the box office. Did they need to talk about those things before they talked about this?

He roved his hands over her bare back and breathed against her hair. "How about we just stay like this for as long as we can?" No outside pressures pulling them apart.

She laughed against his neck. "I'm too heavy. Your legs will fall asleep."

Raising her off his chest, he stared hard into her shiny eyes. "You're perfect."

She smiled but lowered her eyes. "I'm already pretty much naked, Justin. You don't have to lie to see my boobs."

He smacked a kiss to her forehead. "I'm not lying. I think you're the most beautiful woman I've ever seen."

She released a happy sigh and her eyelashes fluttered up at him. "You say all the right things, Congressman." And then she burrowed her face into his neck.

Why'd she have to call him that now? Sitting in the front row of a dirty theatre with a half-naked woman on his mostly covered lap, he felt every bit the picture of a man fallen from grace. But what could he do? With her face pressed against his neck and her lashes brushing his skin, he filled with a sense of peace he couldn't remember having before.

Before Alice, Congressman Mitchell led a life anchored by manipulations. While he worked hard on behalf of good people, his actions were really intended for Robert Parrish to gain power.

Justin didn't want to go back to that—to life before Alice. The trouble was, Congressman Mitchell had a say. He held public office, had family obligations and an increasingly precarious image to protect. In the face of pressure like that, Justin doubted he was strong enough to claim this—claim her. And yet, none of those things made him feel half as powerful as holding Alice in his arms.

Maybe he'd underestimated the strength of Plain Old Justin.

• • •

This was a mistake. Alice squeezed her eyes shut against Justin's neck and fought the waves of nausea that came from weathering her manic moods. She loved him. And this would make it impossible to forget.

His hands smoothed up and down her back, stirring passion mixed with fear. What if she told him she loved him? What would he do? Would he keep doing this, holding her, touching her, making her feel like he loved her too?

She couldn't bear him stopping, so she clenched her teeth in stern warning. *Keep your mouth shut, Alice. Enjoy the ride before life throws you off.*

She'd already been rejected enough tonight. Thoughts of the lost grant mixed with Justin's steady breathing. Without a character to play, she was back to being Alice, and being Alice wasn't easy.

He kissed her shoulder, wrapped her tighter in his arms. On the other hand, being Alice wasn't too bad when she was being treated like this.

But how long could this possibly last?

"Are you hungry?"

She pushed off his chest and studied his half-smiling face. "Are you being…cheeky?"

He laughed and dropped his hands to her ass for a squeeze. "No. I'm serious. Come home with me. I'll cook."

Her forehead tightened with a raise of her brows. "Are you sure?" She'd never stepped foot in his house. How would that look? Congressman Mitchell, entertaining Alice Cramer? And yet, after what just happened, what was still happening, something had changed, a shift in the dynamic that had been so successful at keeping them apart. She didn't feel entirely unworthy anymore.

"Yes, I'm sure. I think we should talk more about this theatre, and what you're going to do next. You're certainly not getting rid of this chair. I like the chair. And the view."

His hands roamed her sides, coming dangerously close to the outside curve of her breasts. "Really?" Her voice caught as he skimmed the skin beneath her arms. "So this is a…business dinner?"

"Serious business," he countered, his mouth inches from hers. And then his thumbs brushed her nipples. "What do you say?"

"Okay." She kissed him to remind herself of why she was willing to risk her heart again. The bottom line, mistake or not, she was going to enjoy this ride with Justin—even if it was the shortest ride of her life.

And in the process, maybe she'd figure out a way to save her theatre, too.

CHAPTER ELEVEN

Justin was a dog person, a statement that had been true all his life. He was partial to coonhounds and anything else with a keen sense of smell and the quickness for tracking prey. It wasn't so much about hunting—Justin hadn't held a rifle since he was a boy. It was more about power, and the respect that came with being capable.

So why in the world was he holding two kittens while Alice poured litter into a box in the corner of his main floor laundry room?

"They are going to be so happy here," she cooed, looking over her shoulder, her eyes melting into a puddle of ocean blue.

That was why. Hell, he was starting to realize he'd do just about anything for her. And that could be dangerous without some parameters. Thank God he had a built-in parameter—his return to Washington.

"What about when I'm back in D.C.?"

She sat on her heels with a huff. "They'll be litter trained by then, and the theatre will be…better. They can stay there without getting hurt. And if that doesn't work, Mouse will just have to deal." She swiped her hands together a couple times. "Okay, let them down."

The minute she scratched in the box, the kittens moved closer to investigate.

Unreal. How could a woman look sexy with her hands in a litter box? Justin shook his head, a little ruffled by the unorthodox twists in his head. "I'm going to make dinner. When you're finished, you can help, but wash your hands first."

She rolled her eyes at him. "Because I needed that reminder."

No, but he did. Otherwise she would've found herself with her back pressed against the laundry room floor.

They would eat first, and then talk. Once they had everything laid out, they could decide how to proceed—with parameters.

Two years ago, he ran on the platform *Plan today for a trouble-free tomorrow.* That was all he was trying to do now. This situation with Alice was…sticky. It didn't mean it couldn't work, it just meant he needed to be careful.

But not so careful he couldn't enjoy himself. He reached overhead to drag the pasta pot off the shelf. If the last week showed him anything, it was that there was a limit to the trouble careful planning could prevent.

He set the pot on the counter and slid it toward the sink. Maybe the best thing he could do tonight was not worry or think too much. The thought alone had him exhaling. He wasn't going to worry about what his family would think—though that was worrisome. He wasn't going to think about where to go from here, because that was complicated. He was going to let tonight with Alice happen. And tomorrow…he'd help her with the theatre and enjoy her company whenever he could before his return to D.C.

This didn't have to be a big deal.

"Okay. What can I do for you?" She smiled at him from the kitchen doorway.

One look at that face and his skin hummed.

It was a very big deal.

Resisting the urge to back her into his bedroom, he concentrated on the task at hand, filling the pot with water. "Grab a jar of sauce out of the long cupboard behind you."

"What? You aren't going to make it from scratch?" she teased as she reached into the cupboard then used her hip to close the door.

"I've never tasted a homemade sauce as good as the one that comes out of that jar."

"That's 'cause you've never tasted mine."

He raised a brow at Miss Nacho Cheese Chips and Cola. "You make sauce from scratch?"

"I can…and I do…"—she said, leaning on the block of granite beside him—"…when it's worth my while."

He couldn't keep his hands to himself, sliding a palm across her stomach and pulling her close. "And when would it be worth your while?"

"When I'm trying to impress someone." She walked her fingers up his chest and pulled apart his tie.

"Are you trying to impress me?"

She grinned and undid his top two buttons. "I think I already did. My lap dance is way spicier than my sauce."

He lowered his head and kissed her smiling lips. "Behind you. Bottom drawer. Grab a sauce pan."

"Say please," she said with a pout.

"Please."

She took two steps, and then shot him a raised-brow look over her shoulders. "You just want to see me bend over, don't you?"

"Maybe," he said, adjusting the burner.

"Tough luck." She shook her head. "You get the sauce pan. It's my turn to watch." When he didn't move she folded her arms beneath her breasts. "Chop chop, kitchen boy."

He liked that moniker much better than congressman.

Chuckling and shaking his head, he walked past her. "Fine. I'll get the sauce pan, but I'm not going to dance."

"I didn't say you had to, but take off your shirt. It looks expensive, and sauce stains." She hitched those lips like a woman entitled to the craziest demands. "And lose the undershirt."

This *was* crazy. Parading around his kitchen shirtless while he cooked. "You can't be serious." He was going to look like a fool.

"I'm dead serious," she said smiling. And then she sauntered over to him and finished unbuttoning his shirt.

His heartbeat doubled. His mouth went dry. He couldn't decide if it was from lust or embarrassment. She slipped her hands over his chest and around his shoulders, dropping the shirt down his arms. Before he could catch his breath, she was smoothing her hands up his stomach, pushing the white T-shirt over his chest.

"You know, I'm normally a pretty conservative guy." Saying it somehow made him feel less responsible for the slip in his reserve.

She helped the T-shirt over his head, tossed it on top of his dress shirt and then turned her hands on herself, unbuttoning the first three buttons of her shirt. "I know how conservative you are. That's why we ditched the shirt and tie."

But it didn't explain why she was ditching hers.

With her arms crossed at her waist, she grabbed at her hem and tugged her shirt over her head, dropping it behind her. Then she bent and snatched his dress shirt. "Seeing you in this makes me uncomfortable," she said, sliding her arms into the broadcloth fabric.

Seeing her in that made him uncomfortable too—in the best way possible.

Her hands disappeared beneath his shirttails, and before he could blink, she was pushing her pants to the floor. Damn. The woman loved to perform. "Is this supposed to distract me from feeling awkward about walking around my kitchen bare-chested?"

She laughed as she fastened two measly buttons on his dress shirt. "Nah. I just like to stir the pot." She crinkled her nose. "Kitchen humor."

He hauled her to him, tired of being teased. "I'm not hungry anymore."

"At least not for pasta." Her brows bobbed and her eyes sparkled.

How had he gone so long depriving his life of this spark? He backed her against the kitchen counter and kissed her…until his phone rang.

Robert Parrish flashed across caller ID. Alice saw the name too.

She squeezed out from between Justin and the counter. "I have to check the cats."

How had Justin gone so long depriving his life of her spark? He looked at the phone again. That was how.

• • •

Alice crouched beside a utility sink that was cleaner and brighter than her bathroom sink at home. Gleaming stone tiles chilled her bare feet as she clutched Justin's cologne-drenched shirt to her chest.

She couldn't breathe. What was she doing here behaving like this with Congressman Justin Mitchell while Charlie suffered in Connecticut, the grant was lost, Harold Parrish was after her theatre and Mayor Robert Parrish was on the phone? Who was she kidding? She didn't belong here.

Sure, she and Justin had some fun in the theatre. But that was her theatre. Her territory. And it was nothing but a distraction from everything that had gone wrong. Now she was here. His territory, a professionally decorated too-many-square-foot house that was occupied half the year because its owner was a United States congressman who flinched at the sound of her last name. Did she really think fun was enough to counter all that?

She dropped to the floor, squirming when the cold tiles bit the backs of her thighs. The kittens crawled into her lap, and she welcomed their warmth. At least they seemed comfortable here.

She still couldn't believe Justin agreed to keep them. It only took her litany of concerns for their wellbeing—traffic in the alley, stray dogs, lack of food, holes in the theatre walls and floors, and Mouse, ready to scare them at home. *Bam!* Justin agreed to take them home and even have them vet-checked. His sentimentality toyed with her heart. He really was a good guy. She wanted to believe that despite the presence of people like Robert Parrish in his life, he'd do right by her the way he was doing right by these kittens.

But that was a long shot—maybe the longest shot of all.

Curling her feet beneath her and filling her hands with fur, Alice hummed the most appropriate show tune she could think of.

"'My Favorite Things.' *The Sound of Music.*" Justin knelt beside her. "You'd never guess, but that's one of my favorite movies. I like when she tells that kid he's incorrigible and he has no clue what the word means."

And Alice liked that Justin could remember such an uneventful part of a film most men wouldn't admit to seeing. She liked a lot of things about Justin. That's what made it so hard to keep the focus on having temporary fun instead of her being desperately in love.

"It's by Rodgers and Hammerstein," she said, focusing on the kittens, feeling strangely crowded by his presence. Once again she wondered what he'd do if he knew she loved him, dreamed of a life with him, wanted so much more than this.

"Robert left a message…nothing important. He wants to form a PAC."

"What's that?" She couldn't look at him.

Justin reached out and patted Oscar's head. "It's…honestly? It's unnecessary." His voice tightened. "And I'm going to tell him that."

Whatever a PAC was, telling Robert one was unnecessary didn't seem like something Justin looked forward to. She could only imagine how hard it would be for him to tell Robert about her. Not that he needed to. Not that he ever would.

Justin stood. "Let's make a salad."

"Am I your dirty little secret?" She had no idea why the words charged out, sounding harsh in her ear.

"No," he snapped, all gruff and defensive. "Why would you say something like that?" And yet he seemed to think about it, his eyes flashing back and forth above her head and his forehead bunching. From the way he sunk his teeth into his lip over and over again, she expected to see blood.

"You didn't answer the phone because you were afraid he'd know I was here." It was the only thing she could think of.

"I didn't answer the phone, because we were in the middle of something a lot more enjoyable."

God, she could kick herself for opening her mouth and chasing away whatever was left of the joy. But she opened, and now she didn't know how to stop, except…

"I should go."

"No." He reached down and lifted her to stand. "I drove you here, and I'm not taking you back to your car until we finish. The water is boiling, the sauce is on, and we still haven't talked about…the theatre."

Right. The theatre. She did come partly for his business mind. She nodded when he nodded, recognition of his mighty fine chest causing her vision to blur. She came partly for his body, too. And that was the part that was getting her into trouble.

"Okay. Fine. We can talk about the theatre." Another mood swing tossed her stomach as she itched to climb her fingers up his chest. "But you're going to need a shirt for that."

He smiled, but his shoulders rose and fell. "I can't keep up with your moods."

"You never could," she said, skirting him and leaving the room. Truth be told, she was having trouble keeping up with them too.

• • •

What just happened here? Justin combed his hand through his hair and stared at the kittens at his feet. One minute he was shirtless in his kitchen, being bewitched by the most amazing woman. The next minute, the same woman was brushing him off. He needed some headache medicine—washed down with a beer.

Alice wanted him to wear a shirt. Ten minutes ago, she removed the ones he'd been wearing. Were they ever going to be on the same page long enough to figure out what was going on between them and where it should lead?

With one stupid phone call, Robert Parrish had messed up Justin's life again, and Justin didn't like it one bit. The man was a meddler. For all Justin knew, he was parked down the block right now, casing Justin's house, fuming because the wrong woman was inside. But Justin didn't care. He was tired of putting his faith in the "right" people only to find out they were "wrong." And if that's what it was like being President, he didn't want the job. Honest to God, he never did.

He was tired of the grand plans and plotting out five to ten years of his life in advance, only to see none of it happen like he expected. For once, he wanted to try focusing on tonight, and tonight he wanted Alice.

But now she didn't want him.

Am I your dirty little secret? The question made him livid. If he were any less emotional, he might stop to ask why. It was a legitimate question, wasn't it? Did he plan to put her on display while he went about congressional business, or was she to meet him only after dark?

No plans, he thought, stalking to his bedroom. There, he yanked a faded T-shirt from his drawer and traded his trousers for a raggedy pair of sweatpants. If he was going to be knocked down every time he tried to get up, the least he could do was dress for the game.

Glancing at the mirror as he crossed the room, Justin grimaced at his hair. He'd combed through it enough to render the style post-apocalyptic rooster, so he snatched a ball hat off his suit valet and slapped it on his head—backwards.

She wanted to talk about the theatre? Fine. They'd talk about the theatre. But there wasn't much to talk about. She needed money. He had money. Talk about a perfect pair. So yeah, they'd talk about fixing the theatre, and then they were going to talk about everything they could do together before the sun rose.

Those thoughts carried him into the kitchen where Alice, dressed in her clothes, pushed up on tiptoes to search his cupboards. Her shirt rode above her waist, and his mouth watered at her perfect, denim-covered curves. Why couldn't this be simple? Three weeks of minimal planning, just a little fun and a lot of sex. But nothing with Alice had ever been simple. That's what made her so damn intriguing.

"What are you looking for?"

She startled at the sound of his voice, dropping to her heels, slamming a cupboard overhead. "Oh. Uh. A bowl. For salad. You said…"

He stood behind her, reaching over her head, brushing her hair with his shirt. The nearly non-existent contact sparked a flame. "Here," he said, setting the bowl on the counter in front of her, breathing her in, stoking the fire.

"Thanks." Her voice was shaking.

Simple static electricity shouldn't have this effect. But it did. And the shock waves urged him to brush aside the hair covering her neck. She shuddered. He placed his mouth on her skin, and she sighed. Every inch of him burned.

"I thought we were going to talk…about my theatre."

"After."

"After what?"

"After we eat." And he sure as hell wasn't talking about food.

CHAPTER TWELVE

Gypsy Rose Lee couldn't help her now.

Alice turned in Justin's arms and came face to face with Plain Old Justin, just a guy who wanted her, Alice Cramer. She could see it in his heavy-lidded eyes, feel it in his scorching touch.

He unbuttoned the buttons she'd refastened only minutes ago, his cinnamon-scented breath steady on her face. While she watched his fingers fumble, she tried to calm her pounding heart. They were really going to take this one step further.

At the beach. In the theatre. They'd gone far, but not far enough. And each time, a pessimistic voice inside her head warned she got more than she deserved. By luck. By chance. Because there wasn't a better option. But now she wasn't quite so sure.

"So…um…" Nervous anticipation made her speak. "What happened at the beach wasn't a fluke caused by too much stress and too little sleep?"

He pushed the shirt from her shoulders and kissed the dip at the base of her neck. "No." He didn't lift his head.

"And what happened at the theatre wasn't just a distraction?"

"No. What happened at the beach and the theatre was… inevitable." His kisses punctuated his words as his hands spread over the cups of her bra, following the lace until he wound around her back.

A quick pinch, a release, and cool air tightened her nipples.

"Like this is inevitable," he said, taking her breasts in his hands, taking her mouth with his.

The cinnamon she smelled moments ago nipped at her tongue, causing a pleasant chill that wobbled from fuzzy head to curling toes. She'd always hoped making love with Justin was preordained, but now that the moment was here she couldn't stop shaking. Silly after what happened in the theatre. But that had been a performance. After her mini-breakdown in the laundry room, she was too raw to be anybody but herself.

And being accepted as herself had always been her biggest fear.

Justin took her by the hand, led her from the kitchen down the dark hall. She had the urge to talk again, fill the silence, help to settle the cells rattling against her bones. But she couldn't think of anything reasonable to say. So she walked…behind him…to his bed…accepting the inevitable.

Inside the room, his hands grasped her waist and guided her to the mattress, where they lay face to face. When he breathed out, she breathed in, his fingers tracing the curves of her shoulders, the swell of her breasts, the tautness of her nipples. Every so often, he leaned closer and offered the sweetest kisses.

She reached out to push the ball cap from his head, so she could run her hand through his hair and bring his mouth to hers to stop his searching eyes, but her other elbow buckled, flattening her on the bed. She bit her lip to hold her laughter. He chuckled for her instead, never missing a beat with the path of his fingers, over her shoulders, down her breasts, across her nipples and back up again.

"I love you," she whispered, her voice breaking the minute she realized she'd said it out loud.

He stopped then. Froze. And a chill wracked her body. Just when she was certain he'd leave the room, return with her shirt, drive her to the theatre and never speak to her again, he crawled over her, placing his lips to hers.

"I love you, too. I think I always have."

She cried, because nothing good, nothing important, nothing like this was supposed to happen to Johnny Cramer's silly little girl. How was it possible?

"If you…"—her voice cracked—"…love me, and I'm not your dirty little secret, then who am I?"

"You're Alice Cramer," he whispered, his lips tracing her jaw.

"But that was never good enough before. How can it be now?"

The mattress jerked, and the pressure of his body released. He settled beside her again, where she could see his face in a sliver of moonlight. His hand went back to tracing her body, only this time starting higher on her cheek, a touch below her ear. He dragged his finger lower to her lips, the tickle causing a shudder.

"You were always good enough." He reached her breasts, and her breath hitched. "I wasn't good enough. I see that now. That's what changed." He leaned over her again, kissing her softly. "I'm going to do whatever it takes to be good enough for you. Starting now."

He tugged on the waistband of her jeans. Through thick, wet emotion fuzzing her head and clogging her chest, she managed to wiggle out of her pants. Justin Mitchell loved her. He wanted to be good enough for her. Starting now.

When his lips nipped at the skin below her naval, she sighed. This was a wonderful place to start.

Telling Alice he loved her obliterated any parameters the congressman may have had in mind, which wasn't necessarily a bad thing. The less of him Justin saw, the more he liked himself. And God, did he like Alice. No, he loved her. He did. He just never realized it until now.

The salt from her skin tingled on his tongue and he breathed her in, memorized her body with his hands. Some things in life came as a surprise without any plan to ease their blow. Loving Alice was one of those things. And it was a blow to everything he'd expected his life to be. He wasn't so blinded by want for her that he couldn't see that. Still, he'd worry about that later, because right now, he had something better to do.

He kissed her inner thigh, and then with his hands beneath her soft hips, raised her body to his mouth. She whimpered, rocked against him, her fingers twisting in his hair. Power rocketed through him, tightening his skin for battle. Every action was bold and decisive, until she broke with a cry. Yeah, he loved her, loved that he could take her there.

And now they'd go together. After all these years apart.

Justin stretched for a condom in the bedside drawer while Alice tugged on his sweatpants, sliding them over his erection, helping herself to every inch of his tortured skin. He shed his shirt, his pants and let her play between his legs, biting back the release he craved. But then she bent her knees and slid toward him in a sultry aggression that broke his resolve.

He wore the condom in seconds.

Before he slipped inside of her, he paused above her, searching her darkened face. So this was it? What he'd wanted for too many years? What he'd pushed away for even more?

"Hurry up," she teased. "We've waited a long time for this."

Yes, they had.

And then the wait was over. He pushed and pulled with his hips as Alice rocked below him, puffing staccato breaths against his neck. The pressure built, tingling in his head, shaking in his arms and legs. If he could bottle this feeling, he'd never feel powerless again.

She moaned, moving faster, her fingernails scraping his back.

He gave…everything. The way he'd always wanted to. No reservations. No rules. She did that for him.

No one else had ever given him something so precious.

• • •

By the time they returned to the kitchen, dinner was ruined. Thick lines of coagulated sauce ran down the colored glass backsplash, while several clumps of the same goo marred the shiny granite.

"We forgot to turn off the stove," Alice said, stepping across the threshold and into the war zone.

"Dang." Justin was right behind her, his hand on the small of her back. "Dinner is going to be delayed."

She didn't care. Her stomach was filled with flutters. Making love trumped making pasta any day. She smiled for the zillionth time that night.

"You think it's funny?" He tossed her a dishtowel. "Try keeping that smile on your face while you're helping me clean."

She had news for him. After tonight, her smile might never fade.

Alice scrubbed at the counter top while Justin swiped the walls. Who knew there was so much companionable comfort in cleaning? Who knew Justin whistled while he worked? She did. Alice Cramer knew things about Justin Mitchell that nobody else knew, like he loved her. She smiled bigger then.

"My mother fired a housekeeper once for a mess like this. Cora Stone. Do you remember her? She was watching a soap opera while the sauce redecorated the kitchen."

Alice's smile fell. "I remember Cora." After Mrs. Mitchell fired her, she was a town joke. Like the Cramers. Once again, the feeling of being out of place buzzed through her, and she fidgeted with the towel, dabbing a splotch of red, scrubbing until it disappeared, wondering who cleaned the Mitchell kitchen after Cora was fired. Maybe Mrs. Mitchell made her clean it before she kicked her out. There was something sick and twisted about the way Alice could relate.

She breathed in through her nose and out through her mouth as she scrubbed, trying not to think about sour Mrs. Mitchell and being the town joke. It wasn't easy. Those were things she'd been dealing with for years. And yet, after the validation of making love with Justin, she was surprised the discomfort hadn't eased.

Sometimes love isn't enough. Her pessimism found its voice again. She couldn't refute it, not when she had her parents as an example. Her father loved her mother, but that love wasn't enough to stop the drinking or the beatings. Her mother loved her children, but that wasn't enough to get out of a bad situation and give them a better life.

And now Charlie loved Morgan, but that wasn't enough save his child.

Alice glanced at Justin, who hummed while he worked. She wanted to tell him all of that, so he could reassure her, tell her that wouldn't happen to them. But she didn't dare. She may know things about Justin that nobody else did, but some unknowns remained. Like how would he react to news that Morgan and Charlie were pregnant and that Charlie wanted to fight for his right to fatherhood? Fights often became spectacles, and politicians didn't like scenes.

Whether he loved her or not, Justin was still a politician, one who would return to Washington. What would happen to them then?

Sometimes love isn't enough.

"Where's your smile now?" Justin dragged the back of his wrist over his forehead, wiping his brow, and grinned. "Hard work, huh?"

"Oh. No." She stumbled. "It's fine. I was just…"

"I know." He moved beside her, scrubbing at a spot on the stainless-steel sink. "You were worrying about your theatre."

The theatre. The grant. How was it possible to not think of those things? But somehow she managed. Orgasms helped. She closed her eyes on the wayward thought. Talk about a night filled with ups and downs.

"I *am* worried about my theatre." It was the truth, without revealing the true reason for her missing smile, so she ran with it. "I have so many dreams for that place. I want four shows a year—two musicals, two dramas." She ticked the numbers on her fingers while grasping the dishtowel. "And I want to start a youth theatre for actors under eighteen. I've thought about letting the drama club use the space, since the high school stage is ridiculously small and half-filled with wrestling mats, which has angered me since high school. And I'm thinking about murder mysteries and dinner theatres, too. The opportunities to exploit a wide-open space like that are endless. I can see it all, the people, the excitement, the success, and my name on the marquee." She took her first recognizable breath since she started speaking, and when she exhaled, her balloon popped. "But I need a lot of money to make it happen."

He tossed the rag into the sink and pulled her close, balancing her on his chest while he leaned against the counter. "I'll give you the money."

Just like that.

She blinked. Could it be that easy?

Justin brushed the hair from her forehead and let his fingers linger at her temples. The tiny circles caused not-so-tiny ripples of warmth to cascade over her skin, and she knew…she couldn't take his money. Especially not after sex. That seemed seedy. Like she planned all along to sleep with him for the sake of her theatre. Her critics would love that. Not that anyone was going to know she slept with him. But he loved her, she loved him, if they somehow moved forward with life under those circumstances wouldn't people assume they had something physical between them, wouldn't they question her motives? She couldn't live with that scrutiny.

"What do you say?" he asked, dipping his head to whisper in her ear. With his hot breath ruffling the curls along her hairline, thrilling every cell, she'd say whatever he wanted her to say…and that was an even bigger fear than public scrutiny. Justin could control her with the touch of a hand. It was the non-verbal equivalent of telling her what to do.

She grimaced, despite the soothing sensations. "I can't take your money. It…wouldn't be proper."

He laughed. "Since when do you worry about what's proper?"

"I do now," she said, tapping his chest with her hands.

"Fine, then it will be a loan. You can pay me back. That's proper," he said as he kissed her forehead and squeezed her to his chest.

But there was more to it, more which needed to be said. How could she tell him what he saw as helping her she saw as controlling her? *Sometimes love isn't enough.*

"We're kidding ourselves, Justin. This is one night, one perfect, wonderful night, but what if that's it. What if this ends…badly?" Like most everything else in her life did.

He pushed her off his chest, cocked his head and studied her face with pinched brows. Just when she thought Congressman Mitchell was going to pipe up and agree, show her the door, give her the boot, Justin relaxed his brows and gave a playful sneer. "Are you dumping me already?"

Dumping Justin Mitchell? It was crazy to think she was actually in a place where she could even joke of such a thing. The thought forced a small smile. "No. Not until after dinner. You promised me dinner." She raised her brows and batted her lashes. "But seriously…" God, she hated being serious right now. And if her father were here, she'd give him a piece of her mind for digging so deep inside her head she couldn't let fun win. She sighed. "If I accept the loan and this…"—whatever this was—"…ends, then I'm stuck making payments to some guy I hate."

He winced. "Stuck and hate are harsh words." His exhale echoed through the room.

She'd finally gone and sucked the fun from him, too. "I know. It's just that happy endings and Cramers don't mix."

Plowing his fingers into the sides of her hair, he cradled her head. "Maybe we can change that."

As if the chance existed…"Maybe."

He dipped his head for a kiss. It was gentle at first, like a silent promise, but when he coaxed her lips open with his tongue, it was a kiss meant to convince. Deep and relentless, pulling passion from her darkest places. When he straightened, he squeezed her again, this time rocking her back and forth. Pressed to his chest, his soft T-shirt cushioning her cheek, she wished the world would end. Then she'd never have to know what happened to her theatre… what happened to them.

"If you won't use my money, then at least use me. I was one hell of a carpenter before they stuffed me into a suit."

She strained against his arms, until she could see his face. "You were a boy, building a tree house for Mark," she said with a roll of her eyes. "And if I remember right, you never finished it."

Lines stacked on his forehead until they disappeared into his hair.

Alice regretted the slight and reached up to smooth the wrinkles, then threaded her fingers through the silk on his head. "My theatre requires man-sized carpentry skills."

He grinned. "Are you questioning the size of my manhood?"

Heat bit her cheeks. "I swear you do that on purpose."

And when he bent down and laughed against her neck, she knew he did.

"Maybe you'd like to see me with my man-sized hammer… witness some nails." As he spoke, he shook his head, pressing his lips to her skin, tickling her with his whiskers.

Oh, she'd like to see him with his hammer all right, but Justin with a hammer wasn't going to fix the bulk of her problems at the theatre. She'd have to figure out something more practical…but not tonight. She needed a break from the seriousness and worry. She needed to concentrate on one hammer at a time.

CHAPTER THIRTEEN

When Justin woke, Alice was gone, but everywhere he looked, she was there, from the smudge of black on his white pillowcase and the lip-stained glass in his sink to the kittens mewling in his laundry room. As he moved through the house he drew deep breaths, expecting to smell her vanilla shampoo. It was like living with a ghost—and he'd only dropped her off at her theatre a few hours ago. How was he going to get through days and weeks without her? Washington loomed.

He squeezed his temples between his thumb and middle finger and wished it would loom over someone else.

After a shower and half a pot of coffee he gave in, allowing himself to wonder what life would be like without splitting time between Harmony Falls and Washington. He had three offices now: one in D.C., one on Main Street in Harmony Falls and one next to Will's in the MCI building. That last one was sorely underused. He wanted a more active role in the family business, but congressional work kept him busy. And this ridiculous bid for the presidency absorbed the rest of his time, pandering to this one, catering to that one. Not even an extra-long shower after party social events could rid Justin of the filth that came along with courting powerful people with questionable motives.

So why did he do it?

He glanced at a picture on the living room mantle. His father was about thirty, dressed in a three-piece suit, standing in front of an American flag. That was why he did it, because he thought it would make his father proud. But did the man even know? The one and only time Justin poised that question aloud, Reverend Miller assured him his father knew. If that was the case, did his father know about Alice?

Justin choked on a mouthful of hot coffee as memories of last night collided with thoughts of fatherly pride. It wasn't that his father wouldn't like him being with Alice—no, Marvin wasn't as much of an elitist as Robert Parrish—it was more like his father would question his intentions toward Alice. Marvin was a deliberate, honorable man—the kind of man Justin spent years trying to be, the kind of man last night proved he wasn't. There was little caution and honor in what he and Alice had done in the theatre. And yet, he loved her. There had to be honor in that.

So now what? She'd asked the same question in the theatre, and he'd brushed her off, preferring to savor the moment without the disapproval time and clarity would allow. He planned to see her again, be with her again, at least until he left for Washington, and he'd see her when he came home on weekends and breaks, but how long could that last before she wanted more, before he wanted more?

And what was more? A public relationship for sure, but a place by his side at fundraisers and family dinners, a ring? He stopped the mug at his lips, knowing he'd never be able to swallow the coffee even if his hand stopped shaking long enough to take a sip. Fun with Alice was a given, but life with Alice wouldn't be so easy. Her flare for the dramatic and propensity toward reckless spontaneity wouldn't win her acceptance in his harshest circles. Even if he could temporarily harness that enthusiasm, some people would never accept her, namely anyone with allegiance to the Parrishes. Funny, that group used to include Justin. Now he couldn't think of anything more gratifying than cutting the strings that tethered him to Robert Parrish. But that wouldn't be easy, either.

Without Robert's backing, could he maintain his seat in Congress? If not, could he make a comparable positive impact in people's lives simply by working at MCI?

He didn't know.

A small scratching sound caught his attention as he passed through the hall on his way to the kitchen. He poked his head into the laundry room where two little faces peered up at him with big blue eyes, eyes like Alice's, so damn sweet one look could cause cavities. He stepped inside and closed the door behind him. Foolish maybe, but work could wait. Hell, he was in the middle of an existential crisis. Playing with a couple kittens was hardly the worse thing he could do.

He sat, suit and all, and let the kittens climb into his lap. His brothers would verbally castrate him if they ever got a look at this.

"Which one are you?" Justin asked the kitten with a smattering of white across his face. He didn't know if the kitten was male or female, but the swipe of color splitting its face into a work of geometric art gave it an edge. "I'm going to guess you're Oscar." The smaller one dug microscopic claws into his lapel. Justin tried to pry her loose, and she meowed. "You do not look like a Hammerstein. There's nothing hammering about you." He chuckled, thinking about seeing Alice at her theatre tonight—with his hammer. The smile that stretched across his face scattered his earlier funk.

Sure, he had worries, but he also had options, which made him luckier than a lot of men.

With pats to the kittens' heads, he filled their bowls and snatched his coffee mug from the counter, determined to get to work. More questions than answers filled his head, but he knew at least one thing for certain. He wasn't interested in the White House, and admitting that was a game changer.

So to whom was he going to make the admission first?

Thirty minutes later, the decision had been made. As Justin pulled into the MCI parking lot, the sun blinded him while perfectly weighted, warm summer air doused his face and Bob Seger blasted his ears. He was on the right track. He could feel it.

After talking with Will, he'd be one step closer to living a life of his choosing rather than one powered by plans from decades past and power-grubbing manipulations.

Out of the car, he took a deep breath to calm his nerves. He might be on the right track, but that didn't mean the track was smooth.

"Morning, Justin," Will's secretary called from the seat of her car. One long leg stretched out the open door and balanced on a high heel piercing the pavement.

"Morning, Georgiana. Need a hand?"

She shifted too many files over the steering wheel to her thigh, snorting when she laughed. "Looks that bad, huh?"

Justin quickened his pace, catching two envelopes before they fell. "Does my brother do any of his own work, or does he stick you with it all?"

She blinked up at him through the glaring lenses of her red-rimmed glasses. "He gives me the easy stuff."

Rolling his eyes, Justin relieved her of the rest of the files. "If this is the easy stuff, I'd hate to see the hard stuff."

Out of the car, Georgiana adjusted her skirt and smoothed her blouse before slinging an equally heavy-looking satchel over her shoulder. "He's got a lot on his plate, what with Mark taking care of your mom and you being gone. It's a one-man-show around here. He's doing the best he can."

If Justin wasn't mistaken, protection laced through her words.

"Well, I'm here now…for a few weeks, at least. What can I do?"

"Ask him. He's kind of a control freak."

That's the Will Justin knew and loved, but what kind of control freak relinquished a good portion of his workload on a clearly drowning woman? Maybe Georgiana was right. Maybe MCI had become too much for Will. If so, then the conversation they were about to have was bound to please them both.

After delivering the files to Georgiana's desk, Justin didn't rush into Will's office. Instead, he walked the long hall in the opposite direction until he reached a cluttered common area. His breath quickened as he maneuvered between stacks of boxes, locked filing cabinets and mismatched chairs. On the other side of the debris, he twisted a knob. Years ago, this was the hub of MCI, and this dark, but oddly not-dusty office belonged to his father. To anyone who didn't know Marvin Mitchell died years ago, they'd think the man was on vacation.

Justin circled his father's desk, the one he used to hide underneath as a boy. With one finger, he traced the woodwork around the edges and tried not to breathe too fast. He hoped his father would forgive him, but after today who knew what would become of the Mitchell-Parrish plan.

"Georgiana said you were here. She saw you come this way."

Justin turned to see Will in the doorway. "Yeah. I, uh, needed a minute."

The whoosh of the air conditioner, forcing cold air through a wall vent, took the place of their voices. For longer than comfort allowed, they stood there, staring at each other, Justin not knowing where to start.

"You look worried. Mom's good, you know?" Will crossed the flawless wool carpet to pat a hand on Justin's shoulder. "Anyone else would've been discharged by now, but when your last name is on the ward, you get preferential treatment." He smiled. "Nothing to worry about."

"What if I told you I wasn't going after the White House? And what if not going after the White House turned into not running for re-election? Should I worry then?"

Will dropped his hand and perched on the edge of their father's desk. He dragged a hand across his mouth and then tucked it beneath an arm slung across his chest. The longer he stayed quiet, the louder Justin's heart thumped against his ribs.

"That depends," Will said, looking straight into Justin's eyes. "What's the motivation?"

"I want to live a different life than the one I had planned." The words escaped in a whoosh. "Robert made it seem like we were partners, like we shared goals, but it was a lie. He wanted a puppet in office, and I let my high-and-mighty principles lead me to the role. But no more. I'm done. So I ask again, should I worry?"

Will stood and gripped Justin's shoulder. "Are you telling me that after this term you could be coming home and working next door to me?"

Justin nodded. "Would you want me?"

"I can't believe you have to ask." Will drew him into a bear hug. "I'd be honored."

Justin relaxed—a little. One admission down. One to go. He hoped the next one ended half as good.

• • •

After spending last night away from home, Alice spent extra time with Mouse that morning. She brushed the burs from his coat, cleaned the guck from his ears and fed him scrambled eggs for breakfast. When he took off after the crows, she took off for her theatre. By the time she pulled into the alleyway, it was almost noon and she'd been over the details of last night a million times.

A million times couldn't dull their clarity or erase her grin.

She hummed as she walked backstage. Eventually the lyrics from *I Feel Pretty* pushed against her lips, and she set them free when she stepped on stage, twirling as she sang her way to the side steps and the orchestra pit. But when she saw the chair from last night, her feet stilled and her mouth shut. Justin Mitchell loved her.

On a giggle, she shuffle-skipped along the center aisle. Sometimes love wasn't enough, but it sure felt like enough today.

Through the double doors and into the lobby, Alice heard a knock on the front door. *Justin.* Her heart slammed against her chest wall, carrying her feet across the ratty floors. If it weren't broad daylight, she'd slip her shirt from her shoulder and flash a little red bra strap. That would start her day off right. But she'd have to settle for something less showy.

She twisted the lock and yanked open the door, her smile plummeting and shattering in the pit of her stomach the minute she saw Harold Parrish on the sidewalk.

"Oh," Alice managed despite her disappointment and shock.

"Little lady." He tipped his silly derby hat. "You look like you were expecting someone else."

"No, I…was in the middle of something."

He nodded, and the up-and-down motion narrowed his eyes. "Can I come in?"

"For what?" Even if Justin hadn't told her about Harold's interest in the theatre, she wouldn't let the weasel in. He was the kind of man who made her skin crawl, the kind of man who looked at her too hard and long, leaving her skin to peel.

"Well, now, don't get scared." When he chuckled, a fleck of something hanging from his nostril fanned in his exhales.

Scared? Grossed out was more like it. As much as she didn't want to go anywhere closer to him, she stepped out of her theatre, closing the door behind her, hoping the message was loud and clear.

"So that's how it's going to be." He wrinkled his bulbous nose, but then quickly smiled, a smile that had the hairs of her neck standing on end.

"What can I do for you, Mr. Parrish?" she asked, keeping her voice pleasant, her breath steady and her shaking hands behind her back.

He looked her up and down in a way that rolled her stomach along with his eyes, and then he settled his beady gaze on her theatre. "This place is a hellhole, little lady. Why not let me take it off your hands?"

It was a showdown. On Main Street. At high noon. While cars drove by and people passed, Harold Parrish leveled the challenge. With her hands shaking and her heart racing, all Alice could think about was not causing a scene. She breathed in and out to calm her anger. She even managed a loaded smile.

"That's awfully nice of you, Harold," she said, stressing the awfully and channeling her best Annie Oakley impression. "But this theatre is all I'm holding, so I can manage just fine." He didn't know that losing the grant complicated things, and she certainly wasn't going to tell him.

His black eyes glistened like frozen earth. "You like being trouble, don't you?"

She wouldn't dignify his question with a response. Instead, she lifted her chin, widened her smile and greeted Mary Clemmons, who was walking her poodle.

Harold followed suit, tipping his hat, but as soon as Mary was out of earshot, he leered. "You want trouble. I'll give you trouble." He slipped a sweaty hand underneath her elbow and squeezed. "How 'bout I drag you back inside, turn you over my knee, and give you some real trouble?"

The contact turned her stomach inside out, and she recoiled from his touch.

"Don't."

Cars rolled past, and she managed to make her clenched teeth resemble a smile…she hoped.

He looked around. "What? You think any of these people would care? About you?" His chuckle drowned the buzz of the workday.

She had news for him, somebody would care, somebody pretty damn important, somebody who loved her. For some reason, the thought stung her eyes, and she blinked in rapid-fire succession to stop the burn. When she did, she glanced across the street at the window four stories above them and wondered if Justin was there.

"Mitchell? You think he cares?" Harold laughed louder. "Aw, honey." He stepped closer and brushed his rough knuckles across her cheek. "Don't be stupid. A man like Mitchell will say whatever it takes to get at what's in your panties." He dropped his gaze below her waist. "But even if there's gold in there, it's not enough to keep him."

Alice cracked. Street or no street, she wasn't going to be sexually harassed and not fight back. She slammed a palm against Harold's face and lunged for the theatre door. She had no idea if he tried to catch her, no idea who witnessed the scene. All she knew was that she managed to get inside and lock the door behind her. She sunk to the dirty floor and waited for the pounding to start, surely he'd want revenge. The thought of him beating down the door caused her to shudder, but even in a fit of rage, she bet Harold could hold his temper better than she could. He'd call the cops instead.

Wouldn't that make Justin proud, watching out the window while Alice was hauled off for assault?

She whimpered. What did he expect? She was a Cramer.

• • •

After a successful chat with Will, Justin decided to ride the positive wave and meet with Robert. Glancing at his watch, Justin determined the meeting was sixty minutes behind schedule, probably on purpose to make him sweat. Justin slipped a finger between his collar and his neck to scratch his humid skin. Mission accomplished.

While he waited he scrolled through emails, wondered what Alice was doing, thought about what he could say to his mother that wouldn't cause the heart monitors to freak, and decided to try harder with Mark now that he was pretty certain the future included coming home to work at MCI.

"Congressman, the mayor will see you now," Robert's secretary said with a bow of her head. She turned on her heels and Justin followed.

He needed to play this perfectly. Robert was mayor of this town. It wouldn't serve anyone to have unresolvable animosity between the Mitchells and Parrishes.

Agnes rapped on the wood door and pushed it open, letting Justin inside. She didn't stay, closing the door behind her.

Robert stood with his back to Justin, facing the hillside neighborhood. His breathing clogged the room until he spoke. "Half those homes are falling down because people don't have jobs that pay enough for upkeep. Do you know what's going to change that, Mitchell?"

Whether it was a trick question or arrogant vibrato didn't matter. "Parrish Plastics, sir." Justin knew how to schmooze.

Robert turned slowly and narrowed his eyes. "Damn straight. And don't forget the role you played in that. Feels good to help those who cannot help themselves, doesn't it?"

He was friendly—too friendly—and the overzealous congeniality picked at Justin's skin, triggering a fight-or-flight response. Words he could've sworn he heard from his father came to mind: *Keep your friends close and your enemies closer.* Certainly his father knew how duplicitous Robert could be. Maybe he spent his whole life trying to do what Justin was trying to do now.

Robert jabbed a fat finger toward the front of his desk. "Sit, son. Tell me why you've been ignoring my calls."

The blood drained from Justin's head. Seconds ticked by as he tried to corral his thoughts. Finally and without certainty, he spoke. "I'm glad we got the plant. It means a lot to our families, but it means even more for Harmony Falls."

"Everybody wins."

"Exactly."

"Then why do I feel like you're gearing up to tell me I lose?"

Justin took an extra big breath. "I've been thinking. What happened at the church wasn't so much the result of faulty planning as it was the symptom of something bigger, something that speaks more to the inner workings of me than anything else…"

"Damn it, Mitchell." He drove a fist against his desk. "Don't give me any of your rhetoric. Spit it out."

With his shoulders back and chin lifted, Justin took the first step toward severing ties. "There's no reason to form a PAC. I'm not running for president."

Robert sniffed, his nostrils flaring. "I see."

But he didn't. Justin could tell by the way he gripped the arms of the chair, his knuckles turning white and then screaming red. He shook his head, offered a few breathy chuckles. "I'd like to say I'm surprised, but I'm not. How could I be after your recent lack of fortitude? First you leave my daughter at the altar…"

"She was sleeping with Charlie Cramer!" There. He said it. No more white elephant in the room where Robert Parrish was concerned.

Robert sneered as he steepled his fingers in front of him. "Are you even, now that you're sleeping with Alice Cramer?"

Justin lunged, slapping his palms to Robert's desk. He'd never felt more rage, more loss of control, more…power. "Don't talk about Alice. Don't think about Alice. Leave her alone." He pulled back just an inch, but made sure his voice didn't waiver.

Robert offered a few clucks of his tongue. "An explosive temper, too. Wonder I didn't see that before. What can I say, Mitchell? You're a disappointment. Looks like you weren't cut out for the job anyway. Too soft. Just like your old man."

The words that were meant to humiliate Justin, elevated him instead. He'd lived to make his father proud. Funny to think that on one of his roughest days, he may have.

Straightening, Justin rolled back his shoulders and nodded. "I don't want to fight, Robert. Can't we just be proud of what we've accomplished together and move on from there?" Was he being too soft now? Maybe, but some things didn't change, and Justin would always prefer diplomacy to war.

Robert's grin was unsettling. "Move on, huh? I suppose that depends on who's moving where. I still have plans, Mitchell, one more that popped up today, actually, and now that those plans don't include you, stay the hell out of my way. How's that for moving on?"

"Fine." Justin nodded. He turned and headed for the door with no handshake or genuine words to give him comfort, just a long silent walk across the navy carpet.

When he exited the building, he drew a full breath. He'd done it, broken the ties that bound him to the Parrishes for too many years.

If he didn't think he'd just unleashed the hounds of hell, he'd have celebrated.

CHAPTER FOURTEEN

Although hours had passed without a hint of trouble, each time the phone rang, Alice jumped, fearing retribution for the slap to Harold's face. This time, when she saw the caller was Justin, she managed a little jump for joy despite her fear.

"Meet me at the alley door in ten minutes." His voice was low and teasing, a tone that skittered up her spine and loosened the stress in her head.

"Did you bring your hammer?"

He chuckled. "You'll have to wait and see."

Ten minutes crawled by as she waited by the door, ear pressed to the metal, listening for sound. Finally she heard the crush of gravel. She threw open the door and saw a pickup truck squeezed into the alleyway, Justin climbing out from behind the driver's seat.

"What on earth?" she asked, taking him in from ball cap to work boots. Lust lightened the air in her head until she felt dizzy. He was gorgeous, every woman's construction dream come true.

"I borrowed the truck from Mark." He walked toward her, his swagger on full display in a pair of well-worn, mouth-watering blue jeans.

"Don't you think you're taking this a little too far?" she asked, her eyes never leaving his body. "All I need is your hammer."

He hooked an arm around her waist and pulled her in. "Oh I brought it. Don't you worry." With a smile, he kissed her nose, and then he cupped her face, dropping his mouth to hers.

Bliss, each and every time they kissed. The bliss rolled over her tongue, slipped down her throat and pooled in her belly, priming her for what came next. Sex. She still couldn't believe they'd gone that far, and at this rate, they were so about to do it again. *But where*, she thought, her inner-director kicking in. There was no bed in the theatre…but there was a bed on that truck.

She smiled against Justin's lips. This time he came prepared, but how prepared?

"It's kind of cold," she said, when he dragged his mouth to nibble her ear. "I hope you brought blankets."

He looked at her then. "For what?"

"The bed. The truck." She felt the flush of embarrassment a second before she heard his laughter.

"That's not why I brought the truck, but I like the way you think." He took her by the hand. "Come here."

Pulling her to the back of the vehicle, he deposited her at the open gate where building supplies packed the bed.

"Oh."

"You sound disappointed," he teased.

She was, for two reasons. "Where'd you get this stuff?"

"Around."

"You found two-by-fours and hardwood flooring lying *around*?"

"Sure." He slipped his hand under her shirt and circled the small of her back.

The pleasant chill wasn't enough to chase the nagging worry away. "For free?"

His hand stilled upon her skin. "Not exactly."

She swatted at his arm and stepped away. "I said I couldn't take your money."

"You didn't take my money. This is a gift. A one-time gift. Consider it a theatre-warming present."

"There's no such thing."

"There is now." He hauled her to him again. "Tell me the sight of that wood doesn't get you excited." He splayed his hands against her bottom and held her tight against him. "Think of what we can do with wood like that…all the holes we can fill."

Screw worry. She tossed her head back and cackled. When they were together like this, it was easy to pretend nothing else mattered. But as her laughter died, she caught shadows on his face. Maybe it was the low light of the alley or the too-little sleep the night before. Whatever the cause, the darkness was there, in the clench of his jaw and the black of his eyes.

Alice smoothed a hand across his cheek. "Where'd you find the time to buy and load this stuff? I know you had a busy day."

He bit his lip, once at first, but then again and again, until it was a full-blown, worried chew. He shrugged. "What can I say? I multitask."

He also wasn't telling her everything. Despite the lightness on the phone and the flirtation when he appeared, something was bothering him. She wished he would confide in her. Then again, she'd had a stressful day, and she wasn't confiding in him.

Maybe if she went first …

"Harold came to see me."

Justin's shoulders tensed beneath her hands. "And?"

"I told him the theatre wasn't for sale."

"Good. How'd he take the news?"

"Not good…" she closed one eye, scrunching half her face. "I slapped him."

"You what?"

"I slapped his face. On Main Street. I'm surprised you didn't hear about it already."

A muscle ticked in Justin's cheek as he gripped her upper arms and held her away from him. She braced for a scolding that didn't come.

"Did he hurt you? Touch you at all? I swear to God I'll…"

"Justin." She laid a hand on his pounding chest, hoping to calm him, hoping to calm her, more than a little shocked at his concern. Sure, he was everyone's knight in shining armor, but it had never been appropriate for him to be hers. "I'm fine. He didn't hurt me. He grabbed my arm, but I was never scared, never threatened. He just said things that upset me."

On an exhale, Justin let her go, stepped back and scrubbed his hands over his face until his fingertips lifted the hat on his head. "I'm glad you're not hurt."

So was she. She was even happier that this conversation didn't go down the road she imagined—with Justin furious at her for acting out in public—again.

"But after the day I've had, after what I did, I sure wish you hadn't slapped him. That makes everything worse." He grabbed his hat by the brim and yanked it off his head, plowing his other hand through his hair.

The alley air cooled around her, and she wrapped arms around her waist for warmth. She wanted to prod about his day, ask what he did, but his feeble insinuation that she'd caused him more trouble pecked at her brain. "So you would've rather I stood there and let the man sexually harass me while he threatened my theatre than stand up for myself?"

"No. That's not what I'm saying. I just…"—he plopped the cap back on his head and crossed his arms over his chest—"…I wish you had handled it better."

Of course he did. She sucked a mouthful of air and swallowed, hoping to break through the shame stuck in her throat. "Again I fall short of your expectations."

"Don't do that."

She laughed for no good reason. "Do you even realize that while you're trying to make things right you're still telling me what to do?"

He hung his head, kicking the gravel at his feet. "I'm sorry."

She'd never been a fan of his tendency to over-apologize, but this time, the apology was warranted. And while she'd have loved to seen him grovel, maybe even admit the slap to Harold's face was an appropriate response, he looked so beaten. "Apology accepted, but you still wish I'd handled things differently, don't you?"

Justin lifted his head and nodded. "Yes, I do. Alice, you can't go around slapping important people."

"Even if they're assholes."

He gave a weak chuckle. "Especially if they're assholes." Two strides and he was close enough to touch. "Those are the ones who'll make your life miserable."

His words resonated with her, causing her shoulders to slump and bringing a sigh of resignation to her lips. "So what would you suggest I do if I find myself in that situation again?" She held up a hand. "Notice the difference here is I'm asking for your opinion, but I'm not giving you reason to think I'll listen just because you told me so."

He smiled, set a hand on the curve of her waist, and the world was right again. "If you find yourself in that position again, I suggest you give a verbal warning, that you won't tolerate that behavior, and if it continues, you walk away."

"That simple."

"Yep."

"My way's more dramatic."

Justin smiled, and the expression lightened the gloom. "That it is."

"I like drama," she teased, more than ready to get back to the flirting.

"I know you do, and that can be a good thing, but you may have to keep it in check. I suspect they'll be more confrontations before this whole thing blows over." The shadows crawled across his face again, but before she could ask why he banished them with another, brighter smile. "Until then, maybe we can make a little drama of our own."

"You're cheesy," she said, wrinkling her nose.

"And you love it."

Alice rested her head against his chest and listened to his heartbeat. "Only 'cause I love you."

"Now who's being cheesy?" He wrapped her up tight like he'd never let her go, but she knew better. Alice Cramer was always one outburst away from losing him.

All the more reason to enjoy it while it lasted.

• • •

Justin tossed another broken floorboard onto the pile of debris. They'd repaired the majority of damaged boards in the lobby, and the physical exertion helped rid him of some excess stress. Enough remained.

Fortunately, Alice was too enamored by the power tools and happy with the progress of her theatre to catch his moments of depressing introspection. He looked around at his work. It felt good to sweat, to create. Of course, someone with more expertise than him would be needed to refinish the floors and return them to pristine condition, but Justin estimated he saved Alice a couple thousand dollars in labor and materials. It was a small drop in the bucket compared to the entire renovation, but on a day when his future worth to people in need was in question, he'd take whatever humanitarian satisfaction he could get.

He turned toward her, finding her on her knees with his hammer in her hand. "Now that you're finished with the hard stuff, why don't you tell me what to do?" she asked, smiling. But it was no innocent question. She dragged the tip of her tongue across the edges of her top teeth.

And just like that, satisfying thoughts and taking what he could get took on an entirely different meaning. He lifted his cap an inch off his head to release some heat. "I thought you didn't like being told what to do."

She touched the head of the hammer to her collarbone and rolled those blue eyes to the ceiling. A deep breath expanded her chest, swelling her breasts against her clingy black T-shirt. "Sometimes I do."

"When?" One word, but damned if he didn't strain to say it.

"When you're dressed like that."

He snickered, momentarily losing his predatory stance to glance down at his work clothes. "You like me covered in dirt and dust and sweat?"

"Actually, I don't like you covered at all, and I bet I can make you sweatier." She slid the hammer down her milky skin, hooking the claw into the V-neck collar, tugging the fabric down.

Inches of shadowy cleavage and a speck of red lace had the orders flying from his dry mouth. "Put the hammer down."

She blinked, hesitated, tugged the fabric lower, but then tossed the hammer aside. It pummeled a newly placed piece of hardwood, leaving a dent. "Oops," she said, batting those lashes, not looking sorry at all. "Are you going to punish me?"

His groin tightened. "Absolutely. Lose the shirt."

She settled on her heels with a frown. "You should spank me."

Those words, spilling from her pouty lips, threw his libido into overdrive. "Lose the shirt, Alice," he growled.

She grinned as she reached for her waistband, rearing on her knees. Slowly, painfully she dragged the shirt overhead. His breathing stopped.

Red lace embraced two beautiful balls of flesh, exactly like he wanted his hands to do. He swept his tongue around his mouth in search of moisture to ease the discomfort.

"This doesn't feel like punishment."

Oh yeah? Then why did it feel like torture to him? "Crawl to me."

She raised a brow. "Like beg?"

"Just crawl, Alice."

Once again, she grinned at his growl. Leaning forward, she braced her hands on the floor and gazed up at him through sultry eyes. "Like this?" Her breasts hung heavy, threatening to slip from the lace.

He swallowed a groan. "Like that."

She crawled, slowly with an exaggerated swing, giving him exactly what he wanted. His erection strained against the restricting denim, while his lungs strained against his restricting chest. When she'd crawled too close to appreciate the front view, he ogled her behind, cradled in cutoff jean shorts.

"Now are you going to spank me?" The crawl was hardly enough to make her breathless, but she was panting just the same.

Up until then he'd never seen the appeal in rough sex between consenting adults, not that he was thinking about having rough sex with Alice, but a little swat to that fine behind was obviously what she wanted. Who was he to deny her that?

With a deep breath and a couple grunts, he managed a painful squat, ramping the pressure in his pants. She completed her crawl, nuzzling his thigh with her cheek, staying on all fours, waiting.

A swallow, and his hand was sliding down her bare back, around the curves of her ass. Sweat beaded over every inch of his skin.

"Do it, Justin," she whispered, and he raised his hand.

But it never landed. Someone else's hand landed on the theatre's front door.

Alice rocketed to a sitting position, eyes wide. "Shoot. Who…" She stopped mid-sentence, like she remembered exactly who it could be.

Justin watched her scramble for her shirt, the knocking coming again, doing a decent job of chasing away his desire.

"What if it's the police?" She looked at him. "You should go."

He didn't move. He felt incapacitated, stuck between the hunger that still pulsed in his veins and the disbelief that there might be legal ramifications to what Alice had done, not to mention social and professional ramifications of being here should she be arrested.

"Go," she snapped.

But he still couldn't move. A new feeling charged his brain. Fear. She said Harold sexually harassed her. What if he was coming back to threaten her again in the same way?

"No," Justin said, pushing past her to the door. "Let me handle this."

"Oh my God. What are you doing?"

But it was too late. Justin threw open the door to Robert Parrish's sneering face.

"Well, surprise, surprise," Robert said. "Or not." He peeked around Justin at Alice. "You kids enjoying your evening?"

Alice pushed in front of Justin. "Good evening, Mayor. The congressman was just helping me out with some repairs."

Robert leered.

"Alice, don't." Justin placed a hand on her shoulder to let her know the jig was up. Robert knew. Or at least he suspected earlier today, and this wasn't proving him wrong.

But Alice stepped away from Justin, moving closer to Robert. "Why don't you grab your things and go, Congressman? The mayor and I can take it from here."

With a chuckle, Robert produced an envelope from his inner jacket pocket. "As much as I'd love to stand here and watch you both squirm a little longer, I have work to do. I came to deliver this. Evening," he drawled without the hint of a smile.

Whatever was on that piece of paper wasn't good.

CHAPTER FIFTEEN

No matter how hard Alice tried to lose herself in the fantasy world of being with Justin, reality found a way to grab her by the throat and force her to face facts. She was a magnet for trouble, and the longer Justin stayed mixed up with her, the greater the likelihood she'd destroy his dreams along with hers.

"Please, go," she said, after closing the door on Mayor Parrish and moving out of Justin's reach. The envelope shook in her hand, and that's where her eyes focused.

"What does it say?"

She saw the shadow of his body moving closer on the hardwood floor, and as much as she wanted to cling to him for dear life, she backed away. "This is my business, my concern. You're getting mixed up in something you shouldn't be mixed up in." She looked at him then, and the lines etched across his forehead and bunched between his brows twisted her heart. He knew she was right. Being with her was a risk he shouldn't take.

"Open it, Alice."

She closed her eyes, too weak with worry to scold him for telling her what to do. "Not until you leave."

"You think I don't have ways of finding out what it is? The mayor delivered an envelope, sporting the town seal. I can make one phone call and learn the contents faster than you can read and process it."

"Good for you," she snapped. He probably didn't mean anything by it, but the words still stung. Her GED and community college degree couldn't compete with his lofty education. After the day she had, she hardly needed more reminders of her inadequacy.

He sighed. "I can help, Alice."

Like he helped by dragging her off to the beach, taking in the kittens, offering her money for the theatre, fixing the lobby floor. It was a long list that would keep growing—if he continued this self-destructive pursuit of rescuing her.

She cleared the sticky emotion from her throat. "What if I don't want your help? In the long run, it's going to get us both in trouble. You don't belong here fighting my battles any more than I belong…"—her throat closed, trapping the rest of the sentence for a second—"…anywhere with you." She dropped her head, and looked at the letter again, hoping her breathing would slow.

"How about you open the envelope and find out what's inside before you worry about fighting anyone, let alone me?" He wrapped an arm around her shoulder and pulled her against his chest.

The voice of self-preservation screamed, *push him away*. The longer she leaned on him, the harder it would be to stand on her own. Another voice whispered, *let him in, one more time*, because if the contents of the letter were as bad as she feared, he'd run of his own accord.

She stayed put, pressed against his chest, and with one finger, she broke the seal. The bold words *Notice of Dereliction* ran across the top of the page.

"They're trying to shut you down, Alice, on the grounds that you've had ample time since the transfer of real estate to bring the building up to code. You need to take this seriously. You need my help."

Her brain sucked up every word he said, pushing hard against her skull, causing blinding pain. She didn't know what was worse, that he read and processed the entire letter faster than she read and processed the first line or that he was once again telling her what to do, and this time she couldn't afford not to listen.

Trapped. At the mercy of a man. Like her mother had been all those years.

He turned her so she was staring at his chest, her arms hanging at her sides, the letter barely between her fingertips, and then he hitched a knuckle beneath her chin and tipped her face so she could see him. "Take my money."

The command made her wince. "I need to think about it—all of it."

"Does that include us, too?"

Us. She rolled her eyes away from his face and managed a shallow inhale. How long had she dreamed of that word? She couldn't believe she was fighting it now. But back then, she never imaged becoming *us* could destroy *them*.

"How can there be an us? How can you want there to be an us? Look at this mess. I've ruined everything." Her lips acted like a magnet for her heart, drawing the throbbing muscle into her throat. "I should've never stood up in that church."

"I wholeheartedly disagree." His thumbs circled her cheekbones as his fingers massaged the base of her neck.

Any other day, the sensations would've driven her gloom away, but today they only served as a reminder of the kind of man she could keep if she was the right kind of girl.

"Robert's never going to back you now. The town, everyone is going to hate me, blame me for putting this rift between you and the Parrishes, and what will your mother think? Oh God…" Her stomach cramped.

He shushed her, wrapping his arms around her shoulders and drawing her in. "I don't care."

"How can you say that?" She pounded his chest, freeing herself from his arms.

His green eyes clouded as he shoved his hands in his jean pockets. "Robert doesn't need to back me now. And this town will get over it. The Parrishes will get over it. My mother will get over it."

The words garbled in her aching head. "What do you mean Robert doesn't need to back you now?"

"I'm finished with politics, Alice. I'll complete this term, but after that, I'm coming home."

A split second of happiness gave way to panic, roaring through her veins until it screamed in her ears. "Because of me. That's all because of me. Because I stood up in the church and started this whole horrible ball rolling. People aren't going to get over that, Justin. You're their golden boy, their great white hope. If you quit Congress after all of this, I'll be labeled the despicable girl who took you down. I can't be that girl."

He stepped toward her. "You aren't that girl. Just because someone says or thinks something about you doesn't make it true. You are who you are. Period." He smoothed his knuckles across her cheek. "I know who you are."

She whimpered. "But I don't know who I am." The last of the panic fizzled in her head, leaving behind an exhaustion so thick she wanted to curl into a ball on the dusty floor.

He grabbed her hand. "How about you try being the woman I love?"

"I don't know who that is. I don't know how you can love me and everything that goes along with me. It doesn't make sense."

"It doesn't have to," he said with a half-smile.

She wanted to believe him, wanted to think the warmth of his hand in hers was enough to answer all the questions pounding in her head, but she couldn't.

Like her daddy said, happy endings and Cramers didn't mix.

He hugged her hard and kissed the top of her head. "You might not want my help, Alice, but you need it. I do not want to see you lose this theatre."

She didn't want to see that, either. She'd lived a lifetime of loss already. She knew she was bound to lose again, but with Justin's money, she could make sure the theatre wouldn't be among the body count.

"Fine. I'll take your money."

And take—not borrow—was exactly what she meant.

At least that way, when they ended badly, she wouldn't have to pay him back.

• • •

Two weeks later, Justin glanced out his office window at the theatre across the street. Since accepting his help in the form of a money order, Alice had entertained construction crews nonstop, and the progress was startling. A few days ago, he watched them raise a new marquee while he conferenced with his aides back in D.C. And today that marquee sported its first message:

Harmony Falls Little Theatre…Coming Soon

He smiled as sirens wailed in the distance. Before long, they blasted beneath the window. In a town this size, it wasn't a sound often heard. Maybe that's why he listened until the screeching faded, wondering what prompted the call. In D.C., he wouldn't have even noticed. Noise was the name of the game.

In a few days, he'd be back in the middle of all that noise.

He sighed, even though his time in D.C. was temporary. He'd be home on weekends and for entire weeks too, but he'd miss the daily check-ins at the theatre, and he'd miss Alice—despite her increasingly puzzling mood. She wasn't happy about needing his money, but he expected her to warm up to the idea once she saw the progress. After weeks of picking paint colors and overseeing sound checks, the best he could call her was flat. Even on nights, when he held her in his arms, her effervescence was gone.

If he thought for a moment pulling his money from the project would put back her spark, he'd search high and low for alternative funding. But he feared it was more than that.

His cell phone rang, rattling his thoughts. He cleared his throat and shook his head, refocusing enough to answer Mark's call.

"Hello."

"Did you hear?"

"About?"

"The Inn is on fire."

That explained the sirens. "Is it bad?"

"Clark told Will it's a total loss. They can't do much more than let it burn while they hose down the outbuildings so they don't catch a spark."

"That's rough. I'm sure they have insurance, but that's not going to cover any money they lose from wedding receptions."

"Or hospital fundraisers. Mom might have another heart attack when she hears about this."

Justin couldn't believe his mother was still insisting on chairing the yearly gala. Of course, after ten years of acting as chairwoman, the gala pretty much planned itself, which wasn't necessarily a good thing. The fundraiser had been losing money in recent years.

"What's the contingency plan?" Justin asked, having never been involved in the planning. That was Mark's territory. He'd been escorting their mother since the year their father died.

"There isn't one. Not this late in the game. We have one hundred fifty confirmed yeses, and no other place in Harmony Falls holds that many people in a semi-formal setting."

The theatre could hold twice as many people. With major cosmetic construction done and current work contained to back stage and upstairs, the lobby would make the perfect alternate location for the gala.

"I may have a solution, but I need to check on something first. Let me call you back."

Excited as Justin was about the opportunity this presented to both the hospital and Alice, he wasn't dumb enough to commit the theatre without her approval. He stood, walked to the window and looked across the street. A couple workers milled around the façade, putting finishing touches on the mortar repair.

Alice was somewhere inside the transformed building, and she wasn't going to like what Justin had in mind. She might even… overreact. The thought of her blue eyes blazing and those perfect lips in a twist, made him smile. He didn't want to fight with her, but he'd do just about anything to see her spark again.

With definite purpose, Justin left his office and walked across the street, greeting people with a generous smile, knowing more than a few believed the stories the Parrishes had been spreading since construction on the theatre thwarted their plans for revenge. A couple rumors had reached Justin's ears. One alleged that Robert Parrish no longer endorsed Justin politically because Justin caused Morgan to have a nervous breakdown. But his personal favorite was that he and Alice had been sleeping together all along. He wished that one was true. He'd learned more about himself from a short time with Alice than he did living in the same skin for thirty-four years.

A worker nodded and drew open one side of the heavy wooden doors. "Afternoon, Congressman."

"Afternoon. It's looking good." And it was. Amazing what money and connections could accomplish in a nominal amount of time.

He stepped into the glistening lobby, breathed in the scent of new carpet and freshly cut wood. His eyes zeroed in on one length of floorboard where despite the mahogany stain, a generous dent cast a shadow. He couldn't help but smile. One of these days, he was going to dish out that punishment.

Passing the grand staircase that led to the balcony, Justin touched fingertips to the cool copper banister. From the rich ruby walls to the mirrored wainscoting, the lobby provided the perfect spot for the town's fanciest affair. And it wouldn't hurt for gossip-happy people to glimpse Alice's vision. His money or not, the ideas belonged to her. It was time people recognized Alice Cramer's positive impact on Harmony Falls.

Her office door was open, but a child-safety gate blocked his entrance. He stood there, watching her work. Sitting behind an ivory and mirrored wooden desk, lush blond locks hid her face enough to block her eyes, but not enough to hide the shiny red lips and long yellow pencil pressed between them. From the open space beneath the desk, he could see her leopard-print heels kicked to one side and her legs crossed. The red paint on her toenails matched her lips.

His gut crunched, building pressure in his groin. As much as he wanted to hop the fence, close the door and spread her perfect body across that desk, they needed to talk. He cleared his throat, and she looked up, pencil between snow-white teeth, red lips curling at the edges. For a second, the sparkle danced in her eyes, turning them a brilliant sapphire blue. But then it disappeared.

"Hi," she said in a soft voice.

"Hi yourself." He straddled the gate, looking for kittens before he squashed one with his big feet.

"I was reading up on script licensing."

"Sounds riveting."

"It is actually. At least to me."

"That's all that matters." He seemed to be saying that a lot lately, trying to get her to see that she was worth the hard work and choices it would take to get this theatre running.

But as usual, her weak smile told him she wasn't sure.

"What brings you here in the middle of the day?" When she stood, the kittens scrambled from her lap.

As she sauntered toward him in a white, sleeveless dress with a thick black belt and bare feet he felt transported to Old Hollywood. She had a way of taking him places he never thought he'd see. He loved that.

"I wanted to see you, talk to you…"—he reached his hands for her waist and guided her the rest of the way to him—"…kiss you."

He felt her body rise as she pressed up on her toes. "What about my lipstick," she whispered just short of his lips.

"What about it?"

"It'll smear all over you."

"I'll take the risk."

Her eyes flashed to the open door, and then she placed a chaste kiss to his cheek before dropping to her heels. "Some things aren't worth the risk."

"Some things are." He shot a hand to the back of her head, tangling his fingers in her hair, holding her still so he could smear the hell out of the lipstick.

When she tucked her hands inside his suit coat and leaned against his chest, satisfaction spilled into every crack and crevice of his body, filling him with an overwhelming sense of right.

He cupped her face and freed her mouth. "So worth the risk. Every damn time."

She grinned. "You look like a clown." And then she was gone, sashaying across the floor to her desk while he wiped fingertips to his throbbing lips. She reached into a desk drawer, pulled out a mirror, a tissue and swayed those hips back in his direction. "Clean yourself up before somebody sees."

Her own mouth wasn't innocent, but he rather liked the proof of his actions being on display. He took the mirror, chuckled at the mess and rubbed his mouth with the tissue until he looked allergic instead of deranged. "Better?"

She tipped her head. "It should get you back across the street without too many stares." Once again her eyes flickered with a flatness that pulled on his heart. He hated seeing it there.

"Did you hear about the fire?"

"No, where?"

"Blue Spruce Inn. It's a total loss."

She frowned and took the mirror from him, walking to her desk. "That's terrible. Was anyone hurt?"

He watched her clean the lipstick from her face. "No loss of life, just property, but lots of people are going to be scrambling for a new wedding reception venue and…"

With a hip perched against the desk, she stared at him. "And what?"

He smoothed his tie, and then tucked his hands in his pants pockets. "The hospital fundraiser was supposed to be next week in the ballroom. My mother and Mark are desperate for another venue, one that holds at least one hundred and fifty people."

She never blinked. "And you think I should hold it here."

"I'm *asking* you if you would *consider* holding it here. I'm fully aware that you may say no, and I'm prepared to accept that." He smiled, hoping to punctuate the playful tone of his proposition.

After a deep breath that lifted her shoulders to bury them in her hair, she nodded. "Fine." She pushed off the desk and returned to her chair. "I'll see you later."

Fine? No, it wasn't fine. "Alice, don't you want to know what the gala involves before you agree?"

"Why, Justin?" she said, dropping her palms to the desk. "If your family needs this theatre to host their gala, then I'm not going to say no. I love you. Besides, it's essentially your theatre anyway. You've paid for all of this."

He didn't want to rehash ownership. This was a conversation they'd had too many times before, and it always ended with her withdrawn, a word that had no business describing Alice Cramer, a woman who was born to shine.

And just like that, his head readied to explode. "You should sing."

"Now?" She eyed him skeptically, the pencil between her teeth again.

"No, at the gala. They should make it a charity concert rather than an auction. The auction loses money year after year."

The pencil hit the desk. "Justin, I…"

"You're singing." Three powerful strides fueled by excitement had him standing beside her. This was exactly what she needed. The chance to step out in front of the entire town and prove her worth.

"And here I thought we'd made progress in the telling-me-what-to-do department."

He dropped to his knees, taking her hands in his, and spinning around her desk chair. "I'm asking you to consider singing for the fundraiser. My family would be grateful, and the hospital would be overjoyed at the boost in funds."

She wrinkled her nose. "How do you know I'd bring in more money than an auction?"

He pulled her down so her forehead rested on his. "Because you're the most amazing person I've ever met, and amazing people do amazing things."

She bit her lip, and her eyes widened.

"What do you say?" he asked.

"I'll think about it." A sassy smile stretched across her face, balling up her cheeks and crinkling the skin around her eyes, but it was the sparkle of blue behind her batting lashes that had him smiling too.

As he knelt there, holding her hands, he knew…he'd been called a favorite son, a congressman, a prospect for president, but when it came down to it, he was nothing without her.

He didn't need a plan to tell him what came next. Following his heart was all he had to do. And if the people in this town wanted something to talk about, he'd make sure their wish came true.

CHAPTER SIXTEEN

Alice had never owned a dress that came with its own garment bag. Now she owned three. Technically, they belonged to Justin. A little pinch of shame picked at her skin, causing her to fidget. Was she ever going to be able to get over the fact that she took his money, having done nothing to deserve it? Probably not. But she'd survived this long in a parentless world by doing what she had to do. This time was no different. Besides, she learned a long time ago that when she hit bottom it was best to lie there until she had the strength to climb again.

With a sigh, she refocused on the vinyl bags lined up on her mama's bed—the only bed big enough for the floor-length gowns to be laid side-by-side. She unzipped the bag closest to the pillows where Mama's head used to rest. Red sequins blinked in a swath of afternoon sun. She traced a finger around the curves of the sweetheart neckline, and then slipped a hand underneath the deceptively heavy fabric, pulling it free from the bag where it could be admired. Her heart fluttered, and she opened her mouth for air.

Singing for a theatre full of rich people who Johnny Cramer once deemed "the enemies" was going to be the hardest thing she ever had to do. She hoped to get a boost of confidence from dressing as though she belonged. Unzipping the middle bag, she smoothed her palms over the black velvet, skirting the rhinestone broach that anchored the empire waist, and then she opened the last bag, careful not to catch the zipper on the fragile silk. The pristine white fabric glowed in the sunlight, causing her hands to tremble. This dress was begging for a stain, but she'd keep it bagged until her middle song set and change into the black gown before she moved into the lobby near the food and wine. That's where Mrs. Mitchell had instructed Alice to mingle. *Mingle.* Cramers didn't mingle. But what was Alice supposed to do? Refuse Mrs. Mitchell? Not when a Cramer was finally going to attend a Mitchell affair and not be relegated to the back row.

The screen door banged and she snapped her head toward the sound. With Charlie in Connecticut and Justin in Washington, nobody should be opening her front door without knocking.

"Hello?" she called, leaving the gowns on the bed and scurrying from the room, closing the door behind her.

"Hey." Charlie stood in the middle of the living room. His clothes were clean. His hair was combed. His face was shaven. A healthy hint of pink played on the balls of his cheeks, and sharpness lit his eyes.

She ran to him, threw her arms around his neck and squeezed. "You look so good."

"Thanks." He patted the small of her back.

"But what are you doing here?" She released him and stepped back for another look at this new and improved Charlie. "What about work and school?"

"I just needed to get away for a few days."

Despite a busy schedule that included work as a line cook and classes at a Connecticut culinary academy, he'd gained weight. Maybe it was the result of being around all that food. But even with a rounder face, the shadowy dips in his cheeks gave away his trouble.

"What's going on?" Alice asked.

"I don't want to talk about it." He shoved hands in his pockets and looked around the room. "Where's Mouse?"

The change of subject saddened her. Over the last month, their telephone conversations had become more comfortable with

Charlie confiding in her about the steps he'd taken to make himself a stable and suitable parent. She didn't know why he wasn't talking to her now. She didn't ask. Instead she answered his deflective question. "Terrorizing crows."

He nodded. "Are you ready for your big show?"

"As ready as I'll ever be. Will you be there?" she asked.

"No." He blinked once, twice and then looked at her, crossing his arms over his chest. "Much as I'd like to hear you sing, that's not my crowd."

"They're not my crowd, either."

He raised a brow and hitched his lip. "They will be…after you sing."

Whether it was a vote of confidence for her voice or a dig at the shallowness of her audience, she didn't care. His comment insinuated that her talent gave her some sort of power, and right now she needed to believe it did.

Her phone buzzed in the distance. "I should take that in case it's about the theatre or the concert, but don't go anywhere. I still want to talk."

He nodded before disappearing into the kitchen.

When Alice answered the phone, Mrs. Mitchell rattled off a new litany of demands.

"Sing *Ain't Misbehaving* to Elliot Price. Walk off the stage and sit in his lap. That man has deep pockets if he's buttered up. I'll put him down front for easy access. And take requests for an inflated donation. I'm still working on the details of that, but be ready."

Now Alice knew were Justin got it. The Mitchell family vernacular was telling people what to do. But somehow Mrs. Mitchell's demands were tolerable. Maybe because she was a mother. Maybe because Alice missed her mother telling her what to do.

"I'll do what I can," Alice said, not making any promises. "My top priority is putting on a first-rate performance so we all have a night to remember."

"I believe we will," she said, ending with an oddly muffled sound.

The stress of the planning so soon after a heart attack was probably getting to her. Not to mention the stress of presenting Alice Cramer to the Mitchells' friends and colleagues amidst the Parrish-created storm of rumors. It still baffled Alice that Mrs. Mitchell was willing to try. Then again, with the change of venue and the added performance component, attendance for the event doubled over last year. Apparently, money was a great promoter of civility.

"It's going to be a huge success," Alice said, smiling for her own reassurance.

"Let's hope so."

Alice had been doing little else. Hope was the single reason she'd made it this far in an otherwise dingy life. She always hoped something bigger and better was around the bend. Now here she was, in the midst of a telephone call with the mother of the man she loved, and all she could do was hope she didn't flub up the gala bad enough to lose him.

"Thanks so much for calling, Mrs. Mitchell." Alice smiled harder, desperate to forge a congenial relationship with a woman she used to fear. "I appreciate your advice."

She ended the call and turned toward the kitchen, still wearing her try-hard smile.

"Not your people, huh?" Charlie stood between the rooms with a spatula in hand. His brows raised in jest. Somehow, he didn't fit the space. Plaster crumbled over his head. Sad-colored paint framed his face. When he'd been drinking, he blended in, but not anymore.

"I'm being diplomatic, Charlie. Sometimes it gets me better results than being dramatic—or overly dramatic." She smiled. "Bottom line, you're my people, and that's my theatre. You should be there." She wanted the world to see what she was seeing.

Charlie Cramer was going to be somebody—just like her.

•••

Justin managed an early escape from Washington, but to his surprise, when he arrived in Harmony Falls, Alice wasn't at the theatre. He drove out to her house, hoping to find her there.

He found Charlie instead.

The familiar man on the inside of the screen door looked different somehow, better, and yet the expression he wore around Justin was the same. Disgust. Mistrust.

"Alice said you were gone," Justin said.

"Yeah, well, I'm back."

"Where've you been?" A part of Justin cared, but mostly he asked for Alice.

"None of your damn business."

"True."

"My sister's not here."

A stench like burning manure filtered out the screen door.

"Damn it," Charlie roared. He turned on the heels of his cowboy boots and stomped into the depths of the house, leaving Justin on the front porch, wrinkling his nose against the smell.

More swearing coupled with banging echoed in the distance.

"Do you need help?" Justin asked, leaning into the screen, careful not to breathe. "Is something on fire?"

Crash. Thump. Clang.

Justin opened the door and stepped inside. Black smoke snaked from the kitchen entranceway. At the ominous sight, Justin jogged into the kitchen. "Is everything o…"

It wasn't the domesticated sight of Charlie fanning smoke out the kitchen window with a dishtowel that had Justin stopping cold. It was the gourmet spread on the countertop where Mrs. Cramer used to keep her fruit bowl. Field greens with walnuts and…where those cranberries? Stuffed mushrooms. Swordfish.

"You made this?"

Charlie used the towel to grab a blackened, smoking pan off the stove and throw it into the sink. "The best part is ruined."

Justin stepped toward the food and leaned in for a sniff. *Heaven.* His stomach grumbled in agreement. "There was something better than this?"

"Dessert."

Straightening, Justin watched Charlie work, rinsing pans, cleaning utensils and rolling knives into a protective case.

"You can cook like crazy. How'd I never know?"

"We haven't been friends in years. There's a lot about me you don't know." Charlie shook his wet hands over the sink before grabbing a paper towel and drying them.

"I'd like to change that."

"Because you're…whatever it is you're doing to my sister."

There was a time when Justin couldn't name what was between him and Alice either. That time was long gone. "I love your sister," he said without flinching.

Charlie rolled his eyes. "Yeah, well, love is sick and twisted. So good luck with that."

With what Justin had planned, he could use the luck. "I'm going to ask her to marry me."

Charlie turned, leaned against the counter and crossed his arms over his chest. He balanced the heel of one boot against the tip of the other. "Does she know?"

"Not yet. It's a surprise."

"What if she says no?"

He'd asked himself that question many times, and the answer was always the same. "Then I ask again and again until she says yes. I won't give up. I can't imagine life without her."

Charlie stared at him, a hard and heavy glare that drew his brows together low on his forehead, and then his nose twitched. "I've been in Connecticut."

"With Morgan." Justin warmed on a surge of contentment at Charlie getting the woman he wanted, but then he cooled a bit when he remembered he once stood in the way.

"Not exactly." Charlie fidgeted, kicked his boot tip some more. "Let's just say I know a thing or two about being shot down and not giving up."

"I'm sorry for the role I played in a plan that kept you two apart, especially if it's making it harder to be together now. Whatever you need, name it. I'll help anyway I can."

Silence swirled between them. As the burnt scent in the air dissipated, so too did the animosity that had been their bosom buddy for years.

"You hungry?" Charlie asked. "Somebody should eat that food."

"I thought you'd never ask."

Turned out the food was every bit as good as the company.

• • •

What a week…correction, what a month, Alice thought, trying not to focus on the ringing in her ears, the fluttering in her stomach and the dryness in her throat. Any minute now, a tuxedo-clad Mark Mitchell would introduce her as the musical headliner for Valley Hospital's Gala of Giving. She swallowed another mouthful of water and stared at her painted toes.

This was the moment of truth. With no character to play and no cast mates to lean on, she'd rise or fall on her own. She breathed in and out, trying not to think about the people in the audience who would love to see her fail. Of course they were there. They'd always be there. But so were the people who wanted to see her soar.

"…I give you an evening with Alice Cramer."

Clapping thundered. Even with the champagne happy hour, she hadn't expected rambunctious applause or errant whoops and whistles. Whether it was sincere or the byproduct of booze, the adulation rattled her, causing her to stumble on her sequined train. Mark flocked to her side, steadying her, and as she righted her posture near the microphone, she looked over a sea of shadowy faces. One smile caught her eye. Justin. In the front row. Beside Charlie.

Her heart squeezed, and then the music started, leaving her no time to think or feel anything that wasn't related to giving the performance of her life.

An hour later, three sets of songs punctuated by costume changes and screen drops ended in the blink of an eye. As Alice sunk into a curtsy, she struggled to catch her breath. *Bravos* and *encores* rose above the applause, and when she straightened, the audience stood too. Justin and Charlie smiled, anchoring the front row, but everywhere she looked more smiles appeared. For Johnny Cramer's poor little girl, the moment was surreal.

A pleasant trill warmed her body as she stepped backward so the curtain could fall.

"You were wonderful, dear." Mrs. Mitchell stood in the wing. Her bony hands clasped at her waist, and her face was void of a smile, but the words came without waiver. Knowing that Margaret Mitchell's approval was hard to come by, Alice happily took what she could get.

Mark's voice boomed, directing the audience to the lobby for a post-performance reception. If Alice thought she was nervous before, it was nothing compared to what she was feeling now, knowing she was destined to mingle with people she'd spent her whole life fearing. What did they think of her now, after the church, the slap and the rumors about Justin? Was a good set of pipes and a three-hundred-dollar dress enough to erase their disdain?

Fifteen minutes later when Alice stepped into the lobby, Barry Beakman grabbed her hand. "Amazing, really, Alice. Superb."

"Thank you," she said, remembering to breathe and smile.

"Darling, if your mother could see you now, she'd be so proud." Beverly Beakman appeared at Alice's other side. The woman sparkled with diamonds befitting a hospital CEO's spouse.

"Thank you, Mrs. Beakman. That means a lot." Alice barely said the words before a tap jostled her shoulder. "Excuse me," she said to the Beakmans, turning to the source of the taps.

"You were breathtaking, Alice. We wish Kory could've been here." Mrs. Flemming wrapped Alice in a hug while Mr. Flemming smiled in agreement.

"Pardon me, miss, can I get your autograph for my niece?" A woman Alice didn't recognize stood nearby. "She's very much into Broadway. I just know you'll be there someday, and I can say I saw you when…"

As Alice accepted the woman's pen and paper, her smile stretched across her face, causing her lips to burn. By the end of the evening, her face was numb, but her smile never faltered, not even when Justin disappeared an hour before the gala's end.

When Mark and Mrs. Mitchell closed the front doors on the last invited guests, Alice collapsed on the bench at the bottom of the stairs. She hadn't realized how tense and hopped up on adrenaline she'd been until now, when she crashed with shoulders slumping and feet throbbing from too-high heels.

And where was Justin? She bent at the waist, unfastened the buckles and kicked the shoes aside. All around her, the cleaning crew buzzed.

"Good night, Alice. Thank you for everything." Dark circles rimmed Mrs. Mitchell's eyes.

Alice stood, her bare feet screaming in protest. But if Mrs. Mitchell was still on her feet a month after suffering a heart attack, Alice had no room to complain. "You're welcome."

Mark nodded. "You did great. Now come on, Mother. Let's get you home." He slid a hand beneath her elbow and tugged.

But Mrs. Mitchell didn't move. She stood staring at Alice, the sparkle of tears in her eyes.

"Let's go, Mom." Mark tugged again.

"I thought you were leaving. Will's already gone." Justin emerged from the front doors. Despite the crisp white shirt, shiny red tie and flawless black suit, his wide eyes and windblown hair made him look frazzled.

Alice's belly nose-dived.

"We're leaving now." Mark pulled again, and this time Mrs. Mitchell moved. She nodded once at Alice, and then shuffled her way to Justin where she brushed a hand across his cheek before leaving.

With her aching feet stuck to the floor and her head spinning, Alice watched as Justin closed the doors behind his mother and brother.

He offered her a shaky smile. "You're going to need those shoes."

She looked at her feet. "Why? I don't think I can subject myself to more pain."

Coming to her side, he wound his arms around her waist and pulled her against him. "You know what they say? No pain, no gain."

Alice blinked up at him. "What gain? What are you up to? Where have you been?"

He chuckled. "Put on those shoes and I'll show you."

With a huff of hesitation, Alice sat again, but before she could reach for the shoes Justin knelt beside her, taking her left foot in his hands. He pressed tiny circles into her arch while he squeezed and warmed her foot, melting her misery.

"You surprised a lot of people," he said, moving his hands to her calves.

Her lips twitched. "Yeah, well a lot of people surprised me. They weren't bad. At all. I guess my dad was wrong about that too."

Justin set her left foot on the ground and picked up her right, repeating the heavenly motions. "I hope your mother's okay. She seemed extra tired."

He grinned. "She's fine. We had a long talk, and she's…good." He reached for a shoe, sliding one heel on and then the other, kissing her ankles before he stood. "Ready?"

She placed her hands in his. "I don't know. You're making me nervous again."

With a wink, he pulled her to her feet. "You have nothing to be nervous about. I, on the other hand…"

She let his words slide, concentrating instead on walking straight despite her burning feet. As he led her out the doors to the sidewalk, crisp night air bit her bare arms and back, causing a shudder. He draped his jacket over her shoulders and held her close, guiding her across the street.

"Where are we going?" she asked.

"You'll see."

A horn beeped. "Congratulations," someone yelled from the murky depths of the vehicle.

Justin waved. Alice smiled. Who knew a small town could be so stoked for a hospital fundraiser?

When she stumbled on the opposite curb, Justin dropped his arm to her waist and held her tighter until she was almost walking on air.

"Evening Congressman. Alice. Congratulations," said a passerby walking his dog.

Justin nodded, and Alice smiled again.

A few feet more, and they were walking into Justin's office building.

"Do you have work to do?" Alice asked, her nerves mingling with confusion.

"Nope."

When the elevator doors closed, he cupped her face in his warm hands and kissed her. Softly. Sweetly. Second after second of breathing him in. Alice floated in soul-deep serenity.

Then the bell rang and the doors jerked open, and Justin clasped her hand in his, moving quickly through the halls. She tried to process the events, focus on the possibilities, but her thoughts scattered.

Finally, he unlocked his office door. "I want you to see something, but first I have some things to say." He spun her around to face him. "I love you, Alice."

She nodded, ready to respond in kind, but he placed two fingers on her lips and smiled. "Wait for your cue," he said.

She lifted her brows in question.

"You'll know it when you hear it." He ran his hand down the length of her arm to squeeze her fingers. "Okay. Let's start again. I love you, Alice. You're beautiful, talented, funny, vibrant and true. There isn't another woman in the world who compares to you."

If she weren't emotionally and physically exhausted, and stricken by the sincerity of his words, she would've argued that last point. The world was a very big place.

"You've shown me things, taught me things that have changed my hopes and dreams," he continued, releasing the pressure on her fingers to grab both of her hands in his. "I don't want to live another day without you firmly positioned as the most important person in my life. So…" He walked backward toward the radiator, dragging her by the hands across the floor. "Will you marry me?"

When he dropped to one knee the theatre marquee captured her bleary-eyed attention. *Alice, I love you. Will you marry me? Justin.* The words shone bright for the entire town to see.

Alice gasped. No wonder people shouted congratulations as they hurried across the street. Her knees buckled, carrying her to the floor where she knelt before him with mouth open, head buzzing and heart thrashing in her chest.

She'd lived her whole life craving attention, wanting an audience to love her. Tonight that wish came true. And yet it wasn't half as satisfying as earning the love and respect of this one man, a man who taught her she was worth the risk.

"Yes."

It was the loudest whisper of her life.

EPILOGUE

Alice paused at the back of the sanctuary, smiling down the lily-lined aisle at the smoking hot man standing before the altar. His tuxedo was tailored, his shoulders were back, and his hair was impeccably groomed. As gorgeous as he was all poised and polished, it was his smile, reaching his glimmering green eyes that made her swoon.

She sighed, smoothed a hand over the snug bodice of her dress and tried to remember a time when she didn't love Justin Mitchell. No such time ever existed.

Suppressing the urge to sprint up the aisle and catapult into his arms, she breathed deep and took in the spectacle around her. The big wedding was Margaret Mitchell's idea, and not surprisingly, Alice resisted at first. Memories of the last time she stood in this spot topped her list for not wanting a replay, but then Margaret took Alice's face in her hands and asked, "Wouldn't your mother want her only daughter to be married in grand style?"

The answer was yes, and so Alice compromised. Big wedding. Big reception. Extra-long honeymoon. Two months to be exact. They could do that now, having waited to marry until Justin's congressional term was complete.

Harp music drifted down the aisle to calm her racing heart. So much had happened over the last year, she barely recognized herself. She'd grown into the woman she'd always hoped to be—proud, respected and loved.

Charlie laid her hand over his forearm and patted her soundly. "This is it."

She nodded, watching the flower girl take her place beside Kory. This really was *it*. The it she'd been waiting for her whole life, since she first saw Justin standing in the doorway of her bedroom. She was drawn to him then like she was drawn to him now. Connected. And while she'd always expected to stay connected but live apart, reality stepped in with a different—better—plan.

The breath she tried to take stuck in her too-small throat as Charlie tugged on her arm. She needed to walk, needed to move, needed to take her place. Beside Justin.

This wasn't the time for puzzling over unexpected blessings and why she suddenly turned out worthy of every dream she'd ever dared to dream. This was a wedding.

The man she loved was getting married.

And this time, he was marrying her.

About the Author

Elley Arden is a born and bred Pennsylvanian who has lived as far west as Utah and as far north as Wisconsin. She drinks wine like it's water (a slight exaggeration), prefers a night at the ballpark to a night on the town, and believes almond English toffee is the key to happiness. Elley writes provocative, contemporary, series romance for Crimson Romance. For a complete list of Elley's books visit *www.elleyarden.com*.

More from This Author
(From *Save My Soul*)

Maggie blinked at the picture she held in her hand. She rubbed her eyes. She tilted her head. She even squinted. No matter how she studied the tattered square, the image didn't make sense.

Her date reached across the bistro table and flicked the back of the photo. "That's my wife and kids."

Maggie counted eight children. A PhD in counseling psychology couldn't guide her reaction. Years of embracing Buddhist dharma couldn't ease her shock.

"I'm sorry." She shook the fog from her brain. "You said ex-wife, right? I must've misheard you." Which wasn't likely. Psychotherapists knew how to listen.

A smile warmed Paul's brown eyes and brought out a dimple in his cheek. Maggie hadn't noticed the deep dip a week ago when he grinned from behind a farmer's market herb stand. She hadn't noticed a wedding ring, either. Glancing at his naked left hand, she felt relieved. There had to be a rational explanation for this irrational conversation.

"Katherine is my wife. We've been married for twenty years." The words leaped from his lips and pinned Maggie to her chair, snapping her bare back against the metal with enough force to sting.

She folded her arms over her chest and breathed, trying to plot a graceful exit from the alternative universe disguised as a coffee shop she must have landed in.

"It's time for another wife."

This was where desperation had led her. But as much as she loathed being a twenty-eight-year-old PhD living at home with her mother, Maggie wasn't desperate enough to escape by way of a married man. She might be liberal, forward-thinking, and even a little off-the-proverbial-wall, but she wasn't a home wrecker.

Drawing a shaky breath, she cursed the crowded location and leaned forward. "I'm sorry. You seem nice enough, but I can't be with a married man. Tonight was a mistake."

She reached into her patchwork purse, but before she fished out keys, Paul wrapped a clammy hand around her wrist. "Don't go. Let me explain. I have Katherine's blessing to pursue you."

"You don't have my permission," Maggie said, uninterested in the details.

He released her and slinked back in his chair, looking very much the misunderstood martyr with glassy eyes and tight lips.

A bolt of pity wrapped in sensibility struck her brain. *Deep breath, Maggie. Calm down.* After all, the evening was innocent. They hadn't even held hands. What harm had been done on a platonic first date?

Compassion caused her to smile. "Good night, Paul. Go home to your wife and kids."

"But I'm a polygamist. I want another wife, and Katherine wants a sister wife."

Maggie widened her eyes. Though rumor had it Salt Lake City overflowed with plural marriages, in the year since she'd moved home with Crystal, Maggie had yet to meet one. Until tonight.

Grabbing the edge of the cold table, she breathed through her nose and exhaled relief. Paul wasn't risking the wrath of karma by proposing an illicit affair. He was explaining an alternative lifestyle. While Maggie had no desire to be Wife Two, she owed him civility and the opportunity to communicate without humiliation. After all, she was an expert in interpersonal communication.

She nodded in understanding. "Please tell Katherine I'm sorry, but I'm not sister wife material. Thank you for the coffee."

Maggie lifted from the seat with as much grace as she could muster and scurried across the tile floor. Her feet wobbled in too-high heels, and her knees knocked below the hem of her flowing skirt. When she finally reached the exit, a cool rush of late October air layered her skin with goose pimples.

She'd been in a lot of ridiculous situations, but this may have topped them all.

Slamming the door of her Aquarius blue VW convertible, Maggie faced the fact that her date was a bust, and now she was going to have to drive home. Face her mother. Rehash the story when all she wanted to do was climb into bed.

This was not the life she expected to be living at twenty-eight. Then again, her entire life had been beyond normal expectations. When most mothers were teaching their daughters to read books, Maggie's mother was teaching her how to read auras. Inside their circle of friends, inside the safe haven of their bungalow, it was a skill no different than rolling her tongue. But out here, in mainstream society, it made Maggie weird, an outcast. She couldn't seem to fit in. Even the men she attracted were…different.

Maggie dropped her head to the steering wheel and groaned. Where was the balance? The ying and the yang? She'd worked hard to gain academic success and respect, in the process, hiding a big portion of herself and her upbringing. And where did that get her? Barely able to pay her student loan interest, car expenses and rent for her office space. This was "failure to launch" wasn't it? She was doomed to grow old, at home, alongside her aura-reading, spell-chanting mother.

But right now, Maggie couldn't go home. She couldn't face the woman who'd be waiting in the rocking chair. Sometimes a girl didn't need her mother.

She turned the key, firing the engine, not knowing where she was going. Her friends were polar opposites—spiritual seekers vs. mental health professionals—and yet both groups would agree Maggie was struggling with self-discovery. What Maggie really wanted was a single friend who would line up shots and drink with her to oblivion.

She drove without direction, listening to the pathetic thoughts in her head until she tired of the wallowing and replaced her thoughts with a mantra. She whispered the words over and over again as she traveled tree-lined streets.

Eventually, her mouth stopped moving and thoughts started forming. The first? She had a decision to make. She couldn't live in both worlds. Either she embraced her mother's way of life or she moved out and carved life on her own. But between student loans, car expenses, and rent for her mostly unused office space, Maggie had only managed to save five hundred dollars since she moved back home. It wasn't enough money for a security deposit, let alone a down payment.

Passing her street, needing more time to think, Maggie guided the car down South Temple and stopped to let a ghost and goblin cross. In the chaos of the evening, she'd forgotten about Halloween. Glancing at her white knuckles, she wished she was younger, with hands wrapped around a pillowcase bursting with candy instead of strangling a steering wheel. Kids didn't know how hard life would get. They couldn't imagine there would ever come a time when they wanted to move out of the house and live life on their own. But Maggie knew, and knowing sucked.

With no other place to go, Maggie parked her Volkswagen in the driveway of a historic Victorian, disarmed security features at the back door and reset the system on the other side. She switched on a chandelier in the main hall and blinked at the brightness. Crystal always said, *look for the bright side*, but Maggie couldn't find a bright side when she was in the middle of an existential crisis.

She growled as she pounded her heels against the hardwoods and took the wool-covered stairs by two. At the east end of the wallpapered hall, she ducked into her office, shutting the six-panel door and driving a bolt lock into place. For a moment, she froze against the thick wood, but then an exhale carried her lanky body to a purple couch. She collapsed, face down on the purple velvet.

Reaching up without looking, Maggie switched on a glitzy lamp and turned her head. She opened her eyes to the Buddha that Crystal had placed against the far wall and the tapestry zafu that was a graduation present from Yogi Hajan. The pair would no doubt advise Maggie to meditate, but she couldn't muster an ounce of spiritual motivation. She looked away before the inanimate objects could guilt her further.

Her orange Macbook sat on the desk where she'd left it hours ago after a virtual therapy session. Maybe one of "her girls" needed help. Somehow it was easier helping other people face their emotional, spiritual, and familial crises than it was helping herself.

Maggie booted the computer and headed straight for Facebook. No new messages. Nothing lurked in her inbox either. Of course not. What sort of college kid stayed in and chatted with her therapist on Halloween night when there were fraternity mixers and costume parties to attend?

She typed a quick email to the small group of clients, detailing her open availability tomorrow. Via email, chat room, webcam or old-fashioned telephone, Maggie would listen to stories of binge-eating peanut butter cups and the bouts of purging that kept the troubled young women up all night.

Pain twisted her heart, and this time the hurt wasn't because of her own screwy life. Virtual therapy allowed Maggie to guide eight clients, battling eating disorders in different corners of the country. The technique was her focus in graduate school, earning her name recognition in scholarly journals near and far. Her avant-garde approach to therapy was something to be proud of, the one and only time she was able to mesh her alternative side with her professional side, resulting in vigorous accolades.

Maggie ran shaky fingers through her spiky hair and considered meditating again, but her thoughts were hijacked by a ringing cell phone. She blinked at the touch screen, expecting to see Crystal or even Polygamist Paul, not an unknown number. The twist of her stomach told her not to answer, but her brain overrode the unexplained nervousness. What if someone was in trouble?

"Maggie Collins," she answered.

There was a brief pause, followed by the deep rumble of a throat clearing. "Dr. Collins, this is Jordon Kemmons. I'm not sure if you remember me."

Her core temperature plunged and then skyrocketed. The skin on her arms pimpled, and tingles spread across her chest. "I remember."

How could she forget? Six months ago, his tan skin, black hair, towering stature, and ominous aura haunted her from behind the podium, where he addressed the graduating class of his alma mater—now her alma mater, too. He stirred such strong feelings in Maggie, she worried the neo-gothic buildings surrounding the commons would crumble after more than one hundred years of steadfast footing. But that was nothing compared to the unsettling jolt of their shared handshake when Maggie was awarded recognition for her research. Something about the darkly handsome man strangled her breath and drained her soul.

"I hope it's not too late to call. I work all hours and pay little attention to clocks and time zones. Can you talk or should we set another time?"

He didn't sound the least bit remorseful for the intrusion, and she had the intuitive feeling that he intended to have the discussion whether she was busy or not. A burst of nervous energy fluttered between her ribs.

"I happen to be at the office, so it's the perfect time to talk." About anything other than late-twenties life crises or polygamists and sister wives.

Maggie ditched her red heels and folded her long legs in the shape of a pretzel.

"You see patients on Halloween night?"

"Clients." How many times had Maggie explained to the layperson about the importance of choosing words wisely when it came to mental health? She sighed and reached for a rote explanation. "The word patient denotes sickness, and my clients aren't sick. They need options and guidance. And no, I'm not seeing clients. I'm doing…inner work."

Silence. She leaned forward, carrying goose-pimpled arms to her knees where her eyes caught the movement of a nickel-sized spider suspended from the blade of a ceiling fan.

"Dr. Collins, I have a proposition for you."

The spider plummeted toward her bare leg. She screamed and leaped across the room, panting into the phone.

"What?" he barked. "Are you all right?" His yelling vibrated her eardrum and flooded her body with foolishness.

She kept her eyes on the spider and one hand over her throbbing heart. "I'm fine. It's a spider." She drew a deep, cleansing breath. "I apologize for my skittishness tonight."

"Let me guess. You believe portals to the other dimension open at midnight on All Hallows Eve, populating the earth with immortals hungry for human souls."

Maggie balked. Was this guy serious? He had no idea how scary real life could be. "Immortals haven't even crossed my mind, Mr. Kemmons. I'm merely distracted with thoughts of polygamy, sister wives and the likelihood of nervous breakdowns in a person's mid-twenties."

More silence. Deeper silence. The kind that made a heartbeat echo.

The spider scurried up the arm of the sofa and then made a U-turn toward the floor. Maggie leaped onto a leopard print footstool.

"Dr. Collins, I'm the agent for a pitcher who flaked out during game six of the NLCS. My sports psychologists can't break through. I don't think he's eating, and I've noticed unexplainable scars on his arms. Obviously this isn't about pitching. The kid is crazy, but his high-profile image makes it difficult to seek inpatient treatment without career repercussions. Remembering your research, I thought maybe you could help."

Maggie winced and dug emerald green toe nails into the cushion, once again taking on the role as champion for the misunderstood. "Mr. Kemmons, the terms 'flaked out' and 'crazy' are offensive. People on a tormented mental plane don't deserve to have their temporary weaknesses belittled."

"Call him whatever you want to call him. I'll call it like I see it. And the way I see it, he isn't focusing. He can't throw a strike, and his fast ball dropped eight miles per hour. I can't negotiate a case of bats for him at that speed."

The spider disappeared under the sofa and reappeared on the woodwork. Maggie dropped her butt to the footstool and pinned her eyes on the eight-legged creature.

"I've exhausted all legitimate, medical treatments," he said with a huff. "Next up is reiki and some cranial sacral voodoo that a team trainer suggested. Before I toss Carlos off the deep end and jump after him, I figured I'd give your brand of hocus pocus a try."

Maggie winced. If he wanted the best hocus pocus money could buy, he'd have to call her mother.

Reaching up to calm a twitching vein in her forehead, Maggie rubbed her clammy skin. "I don't even know where to start," she said, releasing a sigh. "Reiki and cranial sacral therapy *are* legitimate treatments, neither of which do I practice. My brand of hocus pocus…" she choked a little on the words, "…is nothing more than tradition therapy offered in a non-traditional format. I'm sorry to disappoint you, but while I feel sorry for this boy, and not because he isn't pitching well enough but because he's forced to deal with your spiritual retardation, I'm hardly the person to help him heal."

Jordon snorted. "Did you just call me retarded?"

Maggie rolled her eyes, going over her words in her head. "Of course not. I simply meant your spiritual evolution is delayed."

"Is it now?" He didn't sound impressed.

She was beyond caring about impressions. Taking out the evening's frustrations on this faceless man seemed infinitely more enjoyable than beating herself up about it.

With a noisy exhale, Maggie released the frustration that had been locked inside of her since her awkward date with Paul. "Mr. Kemmons, every other word that comes out of your mouth offends me, and that's amazing, because I assure you, you won't find a more open-minded individual than me." She should've stopped there, but the emotional floodgate slammed open. "Just because I won't participate in a polygamist marriage or engage in orgiastic relationships doesn't mean I judge those who do."

Deep laughter slithered through the phone, tickling her ears and neck until it shot off tiny sparks in her chest. She pounded a fist against her breastbone to stop the tingles.

"Orgiastic." The way he said the word made her face burn. "I had no idea that was even a word."

She raised her hand, fanning the heat. "Never mind. I…Good night, Mr. Kemmons."

"Wait," he yelled. "I'm prepared to double your salary."

She didn't have a salary. She worked off billing and sliding scales. It was "eat what you kill," so to speak. And with her brand of therapy in low-demand, Maggie was starving.

"Dr. Collins, are you still there?"

Another shaky breath. "I am."

"Carlos plays for Carolina, and he's staying at my vacation home in Lake Norman. I'd like to pay you for a professional visit.

Talk to him. See if you can help. Travel and hotel expenses will be covered."

For a moment, all Maggie could see was a couple days away from a life that was closing in on her, and some extra cash to start anew. But when she opened her mouth to agree, her stomach clenched. If only she didn't feel like she was making a deal with the devil …

The spider scrambled in the distance, and Maggie scooted the footstool closer to the door.

"Are you interested in the opportunity, Dr. Collins?" he asked in a clipped and clearly exasperated tone.

Maggie had never been one to ignore opportunity, partly because she had her mother's impulsive streak, but also because she was smart and determined…and right now, she was struggling to make sense of her life. This opportunity could be key.

"Send me the terms in writing." She spewed the sentence before she could take it back, using as much conviction as she could muster.

The spider raced toward the footstool, and Maggie screamed, skipping across the hardwoods on tiptoes before she crashed into the sofa.

"What now?" he growled.

"The spider." She panted, waiting for the eight-legged demon to regroup and charge again.

"Kill the damn thing."

"No! That robs us of the chance to grow on a spiritual path. I practice a non-harming way of life, and I'm going to deal with this arachnophobia like any other enlightened adult. When I hang up, I'll talk to him."

Dead silence mixed with the distinct feeling that she said something wrong. Maggie knew the words that made sense to her sounded strange to everyone else—especially tall, dark, analytical men, but she couldn't help herself. Try as she might to tame her alternative thoughts, in times of duress they overruled.

She fought the urge to hang up and handle her mortification in private. "Mr. Kemmons, are you there?"

"I'm *all there*. I was about to ask you the same thing."

She caught his dreadful double meaning, but couldn't blame him. After all, she told him she planned to spend Halloween night talking to a spider.

Palming her face, she drew a deep breath and refocused. "You may think of my person however you like, but professionally, I'm without reproach. I accept your verbal terms and await a contract."

He chuckled. "Good night, Dr. Collins. Give my regards to the spider."

•••

Jordon pulled square black eyeglasses off his face and pressed his head to the scrolled headboard his interior decorator designed for occasions like this. He worked a lot in bed. There was a time when the work related to his libido. These days, the only thing waking him was the BlackBerry charging on his bamboo nightstand or the cordless phone resting in his hand.

A few feet below his bedroom window, the New York City streets hummed, keeping him company through another long night. He bent his knees, bringing the laptop with Carlos Nunez's final stats closer to his burning eyes and pressed the phone to his ear.

The buzzing was displaced by one word, spoken dejectedly with a hint of Spanish accent. "Hallow."

"Hey, buddy. How are you feeling tonight?"

"The same."

Jordon squeezed his lips until they hurt. When Carlos sniffed on the other end, Jordon thought about hopping a flight to Carolina so the kid didn't have to suffer alone. "Is Bernie there?"

"Just left." A yawn filtered through the receiver.

"Okay. Try to get some rest while I work on Plan B." Or was it Plan Z at this point?

Jordon smacked his head against the bed. If he had to, he'd start all over at Plan A and rework every detail until somebody, somewhere, helped this kid. "Night, buddy."

"Night…"

Dad. Jordon couldn't remember when it first happened, but for years now—maybe since he started down the hill toward forty—the name appeared in his head at the end of certain calls. For many of the young men he represented, the moniker wasn't far off. Jordon did more than guide their careers, and he sure as hell felt more for them than the average agent, which was precisely why Kemmons Corp. was anything but average.

Studying the laptop screen again, Jordon shook his head at the numbers. Last season, Carlos flaked out, but the kid wasn't a genuine flake, not like Dr. Maggie Collins.

You may think of my person however you like. Jordon clicked another browser tab and gazed on the exotic Maggie. Betty Boop eyes smiled at him from the pages of her website. He pushed a palm up the stubby underside of his chin, and a devilish grin crept across his lips. Oh, he liked. A lot.

The first time he saw her, she floated down a red carpet aisle, wrapped in traditional graduation garb—with the exception of those damn shoes. It took him a moment to remember he was presenting a doctoral award of excellence to the woman in fuck-me pumps. Later in the evening, at a graduate reception, they shook hands during an introduction, and Jordon momentarily lost his mind.

Glancing at his opening and closing hand, Jordon recalled the heat that travelled from her body to his. The physical attraction intensified when she joined a group in a belly-dancing tribute to an Egypt-bound professor. Having shed the scholarly robe, she wore a sleeveless dress that was little more than a slip. He remembered the generous amount of shapely leg between the hem of that so-called dress and the black bows tied around each ankle. Those tiny bows strapped stiletto heels to her feet as she rolled and swirled all over the dance floor like an erotic dream.

A dream he couldn't shake.

Snapping the laptop shut and tossing it to Bethany's side of the bed, Jordon slid down the headboard, pushed into the pillow and closed his eyes. The right side hadn't been Bethany's side for two years. He thought about rolling over, about reclaiming the space, but his back glued to the mattress. It pissed him off that he still couldn't sleep on the right side.

Maybe Carlos wasn't the only one who needed a therapist.

Jordon launched an exhale from his mouth to the ceiling. If Dr. Collins succeeded in fixing Carlos, maybe Jordon would modify his impression of her from flake to capable flake. The corners of his sleepy mouth lifted. Right now, though, the only impression he cared to imagine was how capable Dr. Maggie Collins was in bed.